Let Me Sleep!

Let Me Sleep!

Anita Raghav

PARTRIDGE
A Penguin Random House Company

To order additional copies of this book, contact
Partridge India
000 800 10062 62
www.partridgepublishing.com/india
orders.india@partridgepublishing.com

Dedicated to

The City of Vadodara—Cultural Capital of Gujarat,

My Inspiration and a place where stories
happen . . .

Acknowledgements

When I started on "Let Me Sleep!" I was not sure how it was going to take shape. Set in a developing city, a normal story of every youngster with common problems, it all came to me just like that.

But the strength of a writer is by the people around—who support and give a pat on the back every time you are inspired. I too, have such a bunch of people.

I would thank Aditya—my very close friend as he shared a lot of information with me and the core plot is around the talks and discussions we had and as he gave a lot of low-down on life at M.S.U.

My special ladies—Riya, Geetika and Keerti who apart from giving me a tour of the University have been great friends and constant support; always chiding me and scolding me if I am not writing.

My parents probably don't even have an idea of the book and might never read it too considering that the genre the book serves is not up to their palette. But I will thank them for introducing me to the world of books and literature. Free times were spent discussing Shakespeare and singing songs from English classics. If not for them, I would probably never have realized my own personal taste in literature and language. They showed the same kind of enthusiasm and energy making me take the first step to presenting the book to the world and I think enthusiasm needs entropy which they have always given.

I have to say countless thanks to many people who don't even know how they have inspired me with their ideologies, the way they talk and their behavior. Each time I met someone new, I have only taken the best from them enabling me to understand my characters better.

I with all my heart, thank Partridge Publications for guiding me through the entire process seamlessly and easily. Two thumbs-up for them!

I want to thank the cities—Vadodara and Ahmedabad; my constant meanderings there inspired me to write about plots located in these two marvelous cities located in Gujarat. The culture, the energy and the very essence of life is most tangible in there and if you are part of it; you are very lucky!

Dialogues

Was I being stupid?

I knew, always, that Rishabh was the casanova that every story sees. I knew that he didn't mean a single word of anything that he said and what he told me or how he tried to impress me was something he had tried on every girl in the University.

But I don't know what made me say 'yes' to his proposal. Now that I am seated alone in my balcony and staring at the streets below, I know the answer. He was very expressive. Even if he meant or not, he made me feel special. His way of expressing it all swept me off my feet and even though my brain was on constant conflict with my conscious, I knew that for once Rishabh wil mend his ways after marriage.

I failed—and that too miserably. I could not grab his attention forever and he has not only left me, he has taken a part of me with him. I wish I had for once more (because I always do) listened to Shiven. Things would have been different and in fact better. And who knows—if Shiven had liked me we would have married. I think I have been stupid on many accounts in life and this is undoubtedly one such. I hope I will be able to recover. I hope I will become the Andy I always was. I hope, I continue to shine like Anuranjini Roy . . .

Anuranjini

How I wish!

I have hated that guy ever since in first year he insulted a senior girlfriend of his. He has no respect for women. I mean he used her because he wanted to clear the exams. Such a sick guy. The first day he tried to sit next to Andy, I wished I could have mauled him with my bare hands. The creature!

I liked her the very first time she grabbed me at the University gates and yelled at me. For the first time I felt like, it's okay to give Vadodara a chance to grow on me. I felt secure because there was someone who felt the need of my presence in the Mass Bunk group and absence from class. I got a sense of belonging and though I knew nobody, that was the day when I began to recognize everyone.

Why Andy, why Rishabh? Couldn't you ever see it in my eyes? What was so special about that fellow? Just because he was singing and making a public display of his affection? Are you sure he will love you like this forever? Are you sure you are not going to be in trouble. I wish I could make you see my feelings, I wish I could tell you, I wish I could stop the clock here. How I wish I could!

Shiven

It just didn't work in my head!

I will never know why my marriage failed. But I know it failed in my mind first and then it came out all. Something stopped clicking in my head. I know Anuranjini never had done anything to annoy me or even ever mention Shiven. But he seemed a good excuse to me for blaming Anuranjini—honestly, in my heart I believe she still misses that Physics maniac more than me. I have seen her glance at their University group photos so many times.

Whenever I saw her with that geek, it boiled my blood that such a beauty with brains was roaming around with an absolute uninteresting person. But why did she turn out like this? She became a typical woman after marriage? I can't believe seeing this form of her. Such a drastic transformation.

I got really put off by her typical behaviour in so many occassions. I guess that is where it came in my mind that in the long run, it won't work. It just won't work and I had no other choice but to call this off. The marriage simply stopped to work in my head as I found flaws in everything Anuranjini did. This would kill her and it would kill me to see our empty relation dragging anyway. I didn't want to be tied down. I wanted to be free again.

Rishabh

#1

Anuranjini had nothing more important work than the report she had to finish before her shift ended. She was constantly typing, making notes, scribbling and talking to herself about the latest reports she had to make. With a last change she closed her folder with a flourish and then temporarily logged off.

'Care for a coffee?' asked Nimesh hanging over her cubicle.

'No thanks', replied Anuranjini smiling, stretching her arms richly, 'I still have some more work to finish.'

'You do enjoy saying no, don't you?' said Nimesh, 'It is just a simple coffee—it won't bite you. Tell you what; I will bring from the wending machine for you even if you don't want to come to the cafeteria.'

'Nimesh please', said Anuranjini, holding her forehead, 'I am having a serious headache. I don't want any coffee.'

'Great', said Nimesh perking up happily, 'Then I will get you some hot tea. It will help you.'

Anuranjini got irritated all the more but didn't reply. She was just too tired and messed up to open her mouth for further argument. She took out her medicines and popped them into her mouth and gulped down water. Just as she lowered her bottle, she saw Nimesh waltzing through the office lobby to her cubicle, precariously balancing two cups and a plate of snack.

'Here I am', announced Nimesh as if arriving from the airport, 'Now have this tea and eat the food—it will help.'

'Nimesh, do you have to overdo things?' asked Anuranjini, suddenly appearing too sleepy, tired and bedraggled.

'I do this', said Nimesh occupying a chair next to hers, 'Because I feel there is something going on with you which you are not ready to speak up. I seriously don't wish to intrude on your privacy and I also don't want to know what's cooking. But at least don't remain lonely. Talk with people around you and you will feel a lot better. I know you won't go talking to people around you. So I decided I will talk to you.'

Anuranjini let out a loud sigh. She felt very happy that there was at least Nimesh in the whole office with whom she could talk. But there were more pressing things turning up and she was not ready for that.

Anuranjini was a normal 26 year old lady with an extra-ordinary appearance. She was heavenly beautiful and perhaps the only beautiful woman—a person without makeup, yet a breathtaking beauty—in her office. She had honey colored skin with curly black hair that fell down over her shoulder. She was a good five feet-six inch and was slim. Her eyes were a strange light, watery brown color, like that of a young puppy. She had a natural aura of an angel walking the earth and she carried herself in a very impressive manner. When she was first recruited, she was the cynosure of all males in the office and there were whispered guesses to her personal life, each guy wanting to grab her attention. Everyone was in the queue to woo her. But she also had a balanced approach and merely smiled when any of the fellow office mates did a good-natured flirting with her. She was also an efficient worker and very soon her work started getting recognition and she got an increment after the probation period. Being a part of the Sales Department of Reginald Corporation, an outsourcing company, was no joke and she was an efficient negotiator. Many of tough and pending deals were cleanly closed and she always came to very good terms with the opposite party. But slowly, she withdrew herself from the crowd and became a general loner and would talk to nobody. Nowadays, nobody remembered her lest it was some work to be done.

'Yeah, I am getting divorced and that has become a very hot topic for discussion in this office', said Anuranjini sipping her tea, 'What to talk with these people, Nimesh? I am sure they don't consider me much and I don't want to be in the limelight once again; this time for all wrong reasons. They got all the gossips about my life—I hope the whole office is happy now.'

'Give everyone a chance Anuranjini', said Nimesh soothingly, 'May be you are just feeling that way. Our office mates aren't that bad you know. Some might be even rational and they might not be judging you. It's only to not put you in a spot—maybe that's why they don't talk.'

'But I am not ready yet', said Anuranjini with a note of finality that hinted this conversation had ended here.

'Can I ask a favor of you?' asked Nimesh.

'Yes.'

'Will you accompany me to the Mall opposite to the office?' asked Nimesh, 'After shift ends?'

'Fine, I will', replied Anuranjini after doing some mental calculations if she had any chore to accomplish.

Their shift ended at 8.00 PM and so the two left for the mall opposite to their office.

There is something about the city of Ahmedabad. It is tightly holding on to the culture of Gujarat, seeped deep in the Gujarati history and preserving the historical virtues to which it has always been an eyewitness—development and simplicity together. It also is on a fast track sprint to establishing itself as the "next big city" and an obvious metropolitan. Though Bengaluru and Chennai have turned to be the I.T hubs of the country—Ahmedabad too is no behind, what with many I.T companies springing up all across the new city, each promising a livelihood to its employees. It is one of the most livable cities and is ready to take in its embrace anyone who wants to be a part of it. The city is expanding proportionally in all four directions and going from one end to another takes minimum forty five minutes.

As Anuranjini and Nimesh stepped out into the warm summer evening—the Ahmadabad traffic jostled around and the entire Satellite area seemed to be illuminating on its own.

It was a working day and so there was no rush in the mall except for few college going students who were loitering there with their loves.

'What do you want to buy?' asked Anuranjini shading her eyes to the blinding golden light of the décor. She had come to any mall in a very long time.

'I don't know', replied Nimesh very confused and pained, 'My sister is coming next week to stay with us for two days. I would like to give her something very simple and sober—not something too much flashy—last time I bought her a dress that was too colorful, she used it to wipe her paintbrush on. She said the dress more or less resembled a rag of colors. That's why I asked you to accompany me. I have no idea and you know how bad men can be at buying stuffs. What do you suggest?'

'You're mistaken', said Anuranjini suppressing a giggle, 'Men aren't bad in buying stuffs if they have to buy it for their girlfriend. But sister—yes! If she doesn't like it, she can say it on your face or throw it away and you might never be able to utter a single word. Sisters have unique powers.'

'What do I do then?' asked Nimesh alarmed.

Anuranjini paused for a minute as she was in deep thought.

'Let's go over to the Ladies' Section', she said firmly.

Anuranjini had a fine time around there shopping with Nimesh as he really proved to be a "bad-shopper" when it came to buying anything let alone a precious gift for his sister. Finally, he bought an I-pod and decided he would feed the songs in—the kind of songs he knew his sister liked, or at least he thought he knew. Anuranjini warned him to be sure of the genre of her favorite music. They had dinner at the mall cafeteria and it was almost 10.00 by the time they were about to return.

'It can't be—Anuranjini Roy!' squealed a voice joyously, so much that the person's voice bounced off the walls of the corridor.

Nimesh and Anuranjini turned to face the concerned squealer. It appeared to be a young woman about the same age as them and she seemed to sprint at a great speed towards them.

She came and hugged Anuranjini as Anuranjini was extremely surprised. She staggered a few steps back as the woman launched on her in a bear tight hug, to get some balance. She was her class mate in graduation and they all were the "cool people" of their college. The two exchanged pleasantries and Anuranjini introduced Nimesh to her.

'Parita', introduced Anuranjini to Nimesh, 'My class mate. We all were one big gang and Nimesh is my office mate.'

'But no big gang over here', said Nimesh smiling, as the two shook hands. 'Excuse me. I got a call.'

Nimesh walked away a bit so that he could talk on the phone.

'So tell me', said Parita, bubbling excitedly, 'After six long years; how is life? And how is Shiven? Do you meet him or not?'

'I have lost contact with him', said Anuranjini, 'No idea where he is.'

'What!' almost yelled Parita; some onlookers scowled at her obvious display of emotion.

'Yes.'

'You both were the inseparable duos', said Parita, 'What happened? How is that you both are not in contact? At least you must be speaking once in a year?'

'No Parita', replied Anuranjini, calmly smiling, 'We both are no more in contact. I lost my phone few months back and so I lost his old number too. That number was anyway not functional. He stopped it long time back.'

Parita was glancing disbelievingly at Anuranjini.

'Anyway', continued Anuranjini, 'After marriage to Rishabh I had to lessen the contacts, right? You know our society—won't breathe properly if a married woman chatted with her "male best friend"—the worst theory being that a guy and girl can never be friends and of course, priorities change. Even he agreed that after marriage we would lessen our talks and chats and contact. So ever since I married Rishabh, I and Shiven never talked even once. I lost my phone and now it's just impossible.'

'Do you want his number? I can ask someone to give', said Parita. She was not ready to believe, 'Even I don't have his new number.'

'No thanks. I won't need it', replied Anuranjini smiling, 'You say; what's cooking on your side?'

The two talked for a while and Nimesh finished his phone call and returned to join them. After ten-fifteen minutes, the three dispersed to their respective homes.

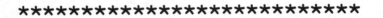

#2

The Maharaja Sayajirao University, Vadodara is one of the most prestigious Universities of the state of Gujarat and the country. Named after the benefactor of the University the erstwhile Maharaja of Vadodara, His Royal Highness Maharaja Sayajirao Gaekwad III, the university buildings speak of the visionary that the great king was. The University has produced some of the finest scientists and researchers for the country and has a huge campus—some courses and institutes spread in different areas and campuses.

The most popular are—The Faculties of Science, Commerce and Arts that are located in the Sayajigunj area—Kalaghoda Circle is a very famous landmark, not to mention the Dairy Den circle that is named after the famous ice-cream joint "Dairy Den" that has served mouth-watering ice-creams for decades to Barodians—starting an ice-cream café culture.

Faculty of Technology is the yet another famous institute under Maharaja Sayajirao University located near the most famous Garba Ground, Navlakhi Compound, near the Maharani Shantadevi Hospital. People for convenience also call it as "Jail Road" as the Central Jail is located some distance away.

The same University is also known as M.S.U—in time some six years back

'What are today's lectures?' drawled Rishabh as he checked out some students passing by.

'No idea. I am not attending', replied Kavya his girlfriend ardently staring at her pink painted nails. It was her duty to look beautiful all the time—she was a fashion icon and many girls did worship her for her taste of clothes.

'Then let's go to Canteen', said Rishabh, 'I am also not attending today's lectures. Today's subjects are all boring. Better to sleep in canteen than in the classroom!'

The pair left for the canteen where the rest of their gang was waiting. They were the group of the most popular students. Everything in the university happened because of them—at least that is what they thought about themselves.

Rishabh climbed over the low step and landed right in front of,

'Manohar Uncle', he said smiling, 'Two coffees and two plates of samosa.

'Kavya?' asked Manohar Uncle, as he stole a glance at Kavya who was still fussing over her long nails.

Rishabh grinned back a devilish grin.

'Why don't you stick to a decent and a sensible girl Rishabh?' said Manohar Uncle, the canteen proprietor, shaking his head disapprovingly, 'Just as a friend I am telling you—do you need to go around with women at all? Why be so reckless?'

'I don't know where that perfect girl for me is Unc', replied Rishabh winking. Though Rishabh had never listened to his own dad, he strangely liked it when Manohar Uncle gave him a fatherly-friendly advice, which still he made it a point never to heed, 'Till then I will manage with Kavya.'

Rishabh Joshi was the college hot shot and any girl on the campus wanted him as a boyfriend. Tall and well built with an appeasing personality that mostly was due to the boyish grin—a thing he knew was his nuclear weapon and he used every time he chased down a girl; he was an apple in the eye of each and every girl in the campus and envy of many boys. He had wavy locks of hair and a dark mole in the left corner of his chin which many girls found attractive.

He took the platter given to him by Manohar uncle and turned when a girl of supreme beauty entered the canteen and Rishabh froze in his tracks. He gave an audible "Oh My Heavens!" as he carried the platter to where Kavya was seated. He seemed to be temporarily transfixed where he stood and didn't know what to do. One part of his brain instructed him not to babble gibberish— beautiful women were a great object of songs and romance for him and he definitely wanted to talk to this new princess.

He put the plate on the table and without even throwing a glance at Kavya, walked over to the girl as if floating in the air. The girl didn't seem to have noticed him drifting towards her because when he came square and sat in front of her and her friend, she jumped and was taken aback.

'Hi', he said giving a hand, 'I am Rishabh Joshi; Third year in Bachelors of Science and Physics department. What about you?'

The girl seemed to be remotely surprised and amused at the introduction.

'Hi', replied the girl taking his hand and smiling as though she was going to burst into total laughter, 'Anuranjini Roy and I too am in Third Year Physics department. Idiot! Don't you recognize me?'

'Heavens!' exclaimed Rishabh, jumping back as though he had received an electric shock, 'What has come over you? You look like some fairy. Did you visit the Disneyland in the holidays?'

'No', laughed Anuranjini, 'I had a cousin's engagement to attend. Just underwent a makeover in the holidays for that. Am I looking that terribly different?'

'Obviously not!' exclaimed Rishabh as if she had spoken a swear word, clasping his heart, 'You are looking like an angel!'

Anuranjini smiled at Rishabh. She glanced at her watch and concluded that the lecture would start soon. She had missed twenty days or more worth lectures because she had to attend a cousin's marriage in West Bengal and definitely she didn't want to miss out on her lectures anymore. It was with great difficulty and convincing had she decided to take leave from college for one month into the new and final academic year.

'I am leaving', she said swinging her bag over her shoulder, 'I have to attend the lectures from today. I already missed a hell lot of sessions during these extended vacations of mine. See you soon.'

'I am also coming', said Rishabh, 'I need to catch up on finishing notes. I can't let myself run short of today's lectures. I will go and get Kavya.'

Anuranjini left the canteen.

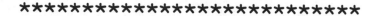

As soon as Anuranjini put her bag down, removed her notebook from her bag and turned, she saw Rishabh occupying a seat beside her. Anuranjini smiled and said,

'This place belongs to Shiven, Rishabh. Please don't sit here; I don't allow anyone to sit here.'

'Come on Anuranjini', said Rishabh stylishly, 'Give others also a chance sometimes.'

'No Rishabh', said Anuranjini smiling, 'This place belongs only to Shiven and nobody else. Please leave, Shiven is here.'

Rishabh cast a disappointed and heartbroken look and left the seat next to Anuranjini. Shiven looked at Rishabh surprised and took his seat next to her.

'What was he doing next to you Andy?' asked Shiven opening his book and flipping to the correct page.

'He wanted to sit next to me because he found me "suddenly" beautiful', replied Anuranjini bluntly, smiling.

Shiven gave an uncomfortable shudder. He had a reason to be so uncomfortable. The whole college knew Rishabh was a bee let loose in a garden full of flowers. Whenever he found any girl breathtakingly beautiful, it took him only less than five minutes to buzz nearby. Since he was the college "hot-shot", none of the girls ever denied his company and were only too glad to have him with them.

That evening however was the doomsday for Rishabh. He and Kavya had an explicit exchange of hollering words at each other at the end of which both split their ways. Shiven and Anuranjini were just returning from their teacher's cabin after some discussion and were deep in the paper that both were holding. They both momentarily stopped and saw the show. Clicking her tongue in disapproval and without throwing so much as a glance at Rishabh's way, Anuranjini with Shiven, left the campus trudging slowly.

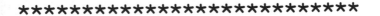

'Stay away from him', said Shiven, 'You have no idea when he will be beside you and then by the time you wink your eyelashes, you would have become his girlfriend. I don't want you landing in the same position as Kavya. Kavya's friends had warned her; she didn't listen to them and now look. The whole college is laughing at her—Not to mention the pain and heartache of a long relationship gone to rags. Be careful Andy, I don't like it. I have this feeling in my bones—It is not a good feeling.'

Anuranjini had called Shiven to ask him some doubt in the topic they both had discussed in their professor's cabin earlier in the day. Shiven could not help advising Anuranjini about the deep sense of foreboding he felt in Rishabh's case. Shiven and Anuranjini were the best of friends, since beginning of college in first year and no power on earth could ever separate the two; the whole college knew that. But Shiven knew Rishabh's history and he was not ready to barter his long term friendship with Anuranjini for petty reasons.

Shiven was the general loner and he didn't mingle easily with anyone in his batch. When he had joined the college at the age of eighteen in first year, everyone around him were happy and peppy about taking admission in one of the most reputed universities. Shiven was the only exception—he seemed to be positively uninterested and remained cool and calm about everything, not involving himself in anything at all.

It was during one "class bunk" idea when Anuranjini spotted him heading towards the college building that she grabbed him by collar and pulled him back and yelled at him for being a spoilt-sport and not being part of the crowd and acting cool and indifferent that Shiven realized that he had spent time in behaving the "lone idiot". He thanked Anuranjini the next day and though Anuranjini apologized for yelling—the two became fast friends since that day and both realized they shared a common love—Physics.

'Shiven I want you to trust me', said Anuranjini, 'I am very well aware of Rishabh's habits and his character. The whole college knows that—come on, he dated three seniors at the same time when we were in first year. I won't listen to that fellow. And *besides; I have a very good friend in Shiven and my passion and love for physics. I don't need any Rishabh or his joking antics.'*

Shiven smiled when he heard Anuranjini. He knew he could trust Anuranjini. If anyone whom he didn't trust; it was himself. At times he felt he became too imbalanced by anger or frustration— either due to friends or studies. It had always been Anuranjini who came, soothed and cooled him down. Anuranjini was such a person too. She was just as gentle and balanced and took ample amount of time with right sense of judgment when it came to taking decisions or crash planning. Given this situation to Shiven, he would become perplexed and don't know what to do. Very soon, he would be swearing loudly. But Shiven had a peculiar knack of sensing deep trouble which Anuranjini sincerely lacked. This had helped both in studies as well as in handling their friends. Shiven also gave a patient ear to anyone who discussed their troubles with him and tried to formulate a plan to help them out.

He was around six feet, fair, with deep brown eyes. Some of the hair around his temples and forehead were curly and he wore glasses with a peculiar kind of frame that made him look cool. He also was one of the brainiest students. The combination was irresistible and many of the girls wished Shiven was their boyfriend. But he never had time for what he called as "teenage gimmicks" and that put off many girls. He and Anuranjini, whom he had christened "Andy", used to spend much of their time discussing syllabus or related subjects.

Anuranjini too was never the beauty of the class. Normally, nobody used to notice her. She was one of those so many thousand girls in the campus. But ever since she had returned after visiting her family for the marriage in West Bengal; she had turned an overnight beauty queen—all thanks to the makeover. Today was her first day and many of the boys had been thrown over by her beauty and Rishabh was the first in queue.

'I know', said Shiven into the mouthpiece, 'Things won't change. Catch you tomorrow.'

Both hung up and Anuranjini was jolted out of her reverie.

'Madam here you are', said the auto-rickshaw driver.

She paid the fare, disembarked and began climbing the staircase that led her to her therapist's office.

She winked her hollowed eyes at the afternoon sun. It was the next day; a crisp Saturday. She was having a half day in the office and her appointment with her therapist. *Everything changed after that day. If I could help, I would just delete that one day from my life; just that one day.*

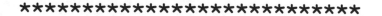

****

#3

Devashish Shastri was packing his bag meticulously. He had a flight to board the next day back to India and he was not in a mood to forget all that he had remembered and bought for his family. It was really tough for him to remember things and buy them. The work had been the most fruitful and the Vice President had promised him a two-month vacation. Devashish Shastri popularly known as "The Big D" had been the part of a research team researching on nuclear and atomic physics. The whole team had a reason to cheer up as the theories ever written on a single atom so far finally seemed to be turning out true. He worked in the Community Physics Research and Development Center at Dehradun and was one of the most efficient young scientists the Center had ever produced. When the Frankfurt Nuclear Research Department had contacted, the Vice President had included his name in the list of short-listed researchers. At that time, Devashish was selected as a junior for the research team. The Vice President never seemed to have repented his decision as he used to get weekly reports and his chest swelled with pride when anyone praised Devashish. He wished that Devashish was his own son. The President's son was now a rave in the

Indian Cinema and stayed million miles away from the world of science his father was so adapted to.

When the team had decided to wrap up the work temporarily for two months—that too after the back-up team had arrived who were to carry on the work for next few months, the Vice President was very glad to sanction him a well deserved break. He had been in Frankfurt for more than a year now and the V.P felt strange without Devashish—always reading, scribbling and talking in loud voices to himself. The V.P and Devashish used to have scientific, good long chats and sometimes thought of solutions to impossible tasks.

The place where Devashish stayed was very sophisticated with two rooms and a kitchen. There were plush sofas with grey and white colors and matching cushions. The curtains matched the sofas with lacey white material. The door opened to the sofas and the first thing that anyone's eye would fall on would be at the telescope perched near the window lentil on the opposite side of the room. There was a huge television which put a doubt whether it was ever watched. The general appearance was clean as a maid made it her personal duty to clean his lodging surgically.

The most striking part of his small home was his little study. Piles and piles of books were stacked around a semi-circle table that held the weight of two U.P.S and three computers. There was an assortment of phones around the table that didn't quite strike as normal phones. There was a huge computer chair. A coffee maker stood in the shadows of the windows. There was a separate desk where lots of journals and handwritten papers were stacked and one pen was constantly lying across the table without a cap. Another huge telescope was perched near the window in this separate study and the far end of the room was lined with racks and racks of books of varied sizes rising up to the ceiling.

The phone went off in the study and Devashish went running there. The phone was from,

'Mom, I remember that. Passport and Visa will be in the jacket pocket. Now for gods' sake don't gather the entire neighborhood on my arrival. I need proper food and sleep and if you insist on visiting variety of temples and shrines; I promise I will leave by the next flight. That is right! What is Malvika doing? I remember everything mom; now don't pester me. I have to finish packing. I will call you after I am through so that I can cross-check. Take care.'

Mothers! He had to finish packing a lot of things and carry some papers back with him which desperately needed his attention.

He was in the middle of perusing through the entire bunch when the maid knocked and then entered.

'Good evening Sir'.

'Good evening Angie. Let us talk business and clear the dues, shall we? I won't be returning for two months at least. May be I will come before that—work is not over yet. I hope you have brought the detailed bill so that it eases me.'

Angie smiled at Devashish. He was such a genius but such a simple thing as calculating daily wages gave him headaches. Angie was a small, middle aged woman and she took care of

Devashish like her own son. Devashish's mother had taken some ease of breath after talking to Angie. She knew how impossible her son could be at times. Angie produced a neatly written bill. Devashish just glanced at it, nodded and smiled,

'I trust you', he said, 'I will just get my wallet.'

'Your wallet is in the cupboard sir', she replied to the back of Devashish who had gone in search of his coat, 'It is not in the coat. You had left it on the table.'

Devashish froze in his tracks and turned toward his cupboard. He brought the money back,

'You are a rockstar Angie. I don't know what I would have done without you.'

'You go home to mamma', replied Angie, 'This place will be ready for you when you come after two months.'

Devashish gave her a hug and she left winking at him. After he had packed and called his mom to cross-check the list; he ate the food that had been already put by Angie before he had returned from the last team meeting two hours back. He rested on the couch and for the first time in so many years a voice echoed in his head: *Laugh at me you idiot. When I will leave you and go; you will be the one who will miss me the most.* There was a ringing laughter. He sat up and then realized that it was just a voice in his head; he shook his head and closed his eyes.

****

#4

'Miss Roy', said Dr. Sridhar, 'You seem to be getting worse day by day. Do you intend to kill yourself by the time you are through with the divorce legalities?'

'I don't know Doc', replied Anuranjini trying hard to keep her eyes open, 'I just can't sleep at nights. Nights have become unspeakable horrors for me. I know my health too is getting deteriorated. It seems ages since I have slept properly.'

'You have lost your appetite too Anuranjini', said Dr. Sridhar, glancing at her through raised eyebrows; 'I don't think this suicidal approach is going to work. Rishabh is living on in his life. You will have to learn to go on without him.'

'Who the hell is interested here to remain hungry and sleepless?' Anuranjini almost yelled, 'My condition is not because I wish it to be. It's just that I cannot. I am sick to the last living cell in my brain.'

Anuranjini's shoulders slumped and she breathed deeply after the outburst. Dr. Sridhar glanced at her sympathetically. He poured out a glass of water for her. She accepted it and sipped it lightly.

'Anuranjini', asked Dr. Sridhar, patiently sitting opposite to her, 'Exactly when is the date of your hearing?'

'Exactly after one week', replied Anuranjini listlessly.

'There is just more to this than a mere tension', said Dr. Sridhar, studying her carefully, 'There is something else that is eating you other than the hearing. Is there something that you have missed? Something important your subconscious knows and is not allowing you to face it?'

Anuranjini sighed and said, 'Yes. I am also suffering a huge wave of guilt.'

Dr. Sridhar raised his eyebrows. He knew more was coming and he hadn't heard it all so far, 'Guilt?'

Anuranjini nodded, her gaze fixed at the glass of water in front of her, 'My best friend Shiven had warned me around six years back when Rishabh had come for marriage proposal that I would be in deep trouble. I knew Rishabh was a flirty character but I always thought boys grew out of it. Boys do; Rishabh didn't. Had I listened to Shiven then I wouldn't be in this mess today. My decision seemed to have upset Shiven perennially. He stopped talking to me and in real senses vanished out of my life. I lost Shiven also—the only friend I had. I have lost Rishabh also. I don't have a husband and I don't have my friend; WOW!'

Dr. Sridhar glanced at the mess named Anuranjini sitting opposite to him. He felt sorry for her and yet he felt that how stupid anyone could get than this. He knew Anuranjini's mistakes were clearly like so many other girls around the globe—serious lack of judgment and absolute foolishness of young age. But this had cost her a lot—for now more than a year, she had become a live portrait of misery and idiocy of the youth.

'So this guilty feeling; when did you realize that you are suffering this?' asked Dr. Sridhar.

'Ever since Rishabh demanded a divorce', replied Anuranjini shaking her head, 'I was reminded of Shiven the first time Rishabh said that. How I wished I had listened to what Shiven had said, how I wish I can go back in time and change everything—How I wish!'

There was a momentary, ringing silence after her words.

'Anuranjini', said Dr. Sridhar, 'All I can suggest you are the exercises I told you of. Somehow I don't wish to give you any temporary healing therapy. You have to work out on it slowly. Therapies can instantly uplift you into a euphoric state but the moment the effects wear out—you might have worse emotional upheaval. You need to come out of it slowly and naturally. Have you joined any hobby classes?'

'No', said Anuranjini, 'I am going to the library though. Reading keeps me fresh.'

Dr. Sridhar nodded. They talked for another hour and then thanking him, Anuranjini left.

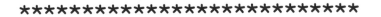

'You are late', whimpered a young lady of around twenty-three who was waiting at the Mc Donald's.

'Sorry gorgeous', said Rishabh, smiling and coming with a bunch of red roses, 'I had a meeting and it took ten minutes extra of the lunch break. I also had to get you the best roses in the whole city.'

'Thanks', said the girl smiling and accepting the huge bunch of roses.

'So Madhvi', said Rishabh, 'How is office going?'

'Tough. But I like the work load. It keeps me busy', said Madhvi tossing the flowers on the chair beside her. Madhvi was now so much used to the amount of variety flowers Rishabh gave her—she loved being pampered.

A girl was sitting at the adjacent table with her head down. She raised her head and Rishabh's eyes fell on her. He gave a mean smile and saying an excuse to Madhvi went over to her.

'Anuranjini', he said occupying the seat, opposite to her, 'I really feel sorry for you.'

There was lot of meanness in the way he was speaking and Anuranjini knew, her soon-going-to-be-ex husband was trying to create a scene just like he had done before by coming to her office. She knew he was trying to make her miserable but she wasn't going to give him that luxury.

Anuranjini glanced at him wearily and smiled, 'Don't. I don't feel sorry for myself. I don't need your sympathy.'

'I wish this marriage had worked', said Rishabh without any emotion, but a wicked smile played around his mouth.

'I don't know about this marriage', said Anuranjini scornfully, glancing over at Madhvi, 'But I seriously hope your next marriage works. I see that you have got a new flower to suck nectar from.'

Rishabh smiled evilly.

'You know what', said Anuranjini carefully choosing her next words so that she could hit the mark, 'Everyone around me always knew you are an inscrutable jerk—specifically Shiven.'

Rishabh's smile faded at the tone in which Anuranjini spoke and on top of that she took Shiven's name. For Rishabh, the name "Shiven" was not less than any swear word. Taking Shiven's name in his presence was like punching him in the stomach.

'Everyone had warned me about you including him', continued Anuranjini smiling triumphantly, 'But I was the big hearted girl in the whole world and decided to give you a chance. I am glad that we are getting divorced because that would only prove everyone correct and me wrong. And I have never been so happy in my life on being proven wrong, trust me. I don't care a damn about you. So I suggest you dear husband, stay away from me and don't try to rag me like you used to do sometimes at the university college hostel. I know one thing for sure; I am better off without you. Thank you for leaving me forever.'

Rishabh's temper gave away. He grabbed a glass and banged it on the table which exploded into shards. He did this slowly so that he didn't attract attention but the waiter saw him and cringed.

'See', smiled Anuranjini scornfully, 'You are weaker than me. I feel sorry for you darling.'

She motioned to the waiter and smiled, 'Here is the tip you deserve; also, the extra for the glass. Keep the change', and with one swish of her handbag left the restaurant.

Rishabh was seething in anger—he wanted to make her miserable and he ended being miserable.

****

#5

The wait at the Chhatrapati Shivaji International Airport was the painful part and Devashish was not at all in a mood to wait. His eyes were red and he wanted to get some good sleep. Though he had slept on the flight nothing could replace the joy of a comfortable bed at home. He had to catch a connecting flight in the evening back home. The Mumbai airport seemed to be swelling with people day by day and he was fed up of the noise and people walking, talking and the echoes that magnified every sound. He decided to call up at home. After staying for almost two years away from his country, he felt strangely detached from his own people. It was as if he didn't know them and that he had landed onto an altogether a different planet.

He made the call and returned to a food counter to grab a coffee and a sandwich. He didn't like the taste but nevertheless he rammed the food down the throat and forced it to work.

Why Devashish; what has happened to you? said a voice. He felt his own inner self reflecting back at him from the clean glass wall; *Haven't you escaped enough? You ran away from home to Dehradun and from there to Frankfurt. Are you planning to run like this? Running for studies isn't that good a practice. Trust me with this rate you can participate in the next Olympics.*

Devashish angrily glanced at his own reflection. His inner self was smiling back at him—or so he thought.

You are so damn scared of yourself that you don't even know that this running is going to cost you a lot. You could have continued this staying at home. But you were forever that airplane that didn't know to land when it came to life. Always remember something Devashish Shastri, if you get scared of yourself or me for that reason, you will have no one to escape to. You can hide the goddamn truth from the whole world but not me. Just grow up young man! This is just the beginning of your journey—as a scientist. More secrets are yet to be unveiled.

Devashish ran down to the bathroom and opened up the tap. He wet a tissue and wiped his face. He didn't want to glance up at himself in the mirror. He was getting perplexed to hear his own voice eerily reverberate inside his own head. He decided he was being stupid and that he would buy a book and busy himself: *Inner self and rubbish!* And that is what he did; he bought a book and poured into it.

More books! Remarked someone inside him. He scowled to himself.

He was at the domestic air terminus and waited till his flight was announced. Never had he felt so jubilant when his security check was declared. He was tired and he was scared of being alone. He just wanted to be home and bring some rest to the inner self that was pinching and poking him.

He chided himself: *Shut your brain up Devu! Forget it, Forget it!*

★★★★★★★★★★★★★★★★★★★★★★★★★

#6

The Maharaja Sayajirao University, Vadodara—Six years behind in time—One of the shady avenues outside the Physics Department.

Anuranjini: *Shiven, there is something wrong. I tried all the methods and replaced many constants. The answer has decided it won't come to me. The numerical has won the war against me! I spent whole three hours in the night trying to solve it. Now, will you try it out for gods' sake? Because I don't want to hear a "No" for answer!*

Shiven: *Will you be patient? It won't pay if you lose temper over it. This is Physics! And who asked you to lose three hours of sleep? If the answer comes in one shot, it will come—else it won't. I thought you knew the rule.*

Anuranjini yawned richly, masking her mouth, scowled and rubbed her eyes and when she opened it; there stood Rishabh in front of her.

Anuranjini *(bored and uninterested):* What?

Rishabh: *Hey Gorgeous! Don't stress out too much on Physics. This is just a subject.*

Shiven (*Still deep in the sum*): *Go away from here Rish, I don't want trouble right now. We both are trying to solve this out. If you ever stepped into the class then only will you realize that this is Physics.*

Rishabh: *Oh come on Mr. Handsome Geek; just chill. Physics won't fill your tummy.*

Shiven: *So won't loitering. If you are not here to help us, at least you can do us a favor and leave.*

Rishabh: *Look dude, I came here to meet Andy.*

Shiven (*Looking up angrily*): *Only I call her Andy; don't you call her Andy. This is my personal copyright. You stick to Anuranjini while you are here and better off you will be if you don't stick around at all.*

Rishabh came on to his feet. Shiven realizing it was fighting time stood up and rose to his full height. Somehow he seemed to overshadow Rishabh and he had a quiet piercing gaze that seemed to counter—soften up Rishabh's anger. The scene was so melodramatic a minute that no one knew who was stronger; the silent and unwavering Shiven or the ready to attack, energetic Rishabh. Everyone realizing they could expect a scene right out of a Hindi movie gathered around.

Shiven: *Look Rish. I seriously don't want trouble. The whole campus is watching and I don't want to make a hole in you. Just leave me and Andy alone and you will be absolutely fine.*

Rishabh: *And what if I don't?*

There was a sound of a huge smack as Shiven slapped Rishabh and Rishabh was on the ground.

The crowd gasped for no one had ever seen the calm and silent studious boy Shiven lose his temper.

Shiven (venomously): I had warned you.

Anuranjini (Shocked): Shiven! Why the heck did you use your hand on him? Come on let's leave. Please!

Anuranjini ran forward and gave her hand to Rishabh and helped him on foot. Muttering a quick apology she dragged Shiven away from launching on Rishabh. The campus had temporarily frozen on seeing the scene.

★★★★★★★★★★★★★★★★★★★★★★★★★

'What's wrong with you Shiven?' burst out Anuranjini when they were near the Auditorium, 'Who the holy heavens on earth asked you to hit him?'

In absolute fury, Shiven had walked the entire length till the C.C. Mehta Auditorium where both had parked their vehicles. He wanted to break lot of things, blast glass into pieces and say swear words loudly. He was aware of Anuranjini calling him and running to keep up with him.

'He is an irritating chap and I hate him', wheezed Shiven; partly because of anger and partly because of being dragged away by Anuranjini.

'He hasn't done any damage to us Shiven; what is going on in your mind?' asked Anuranjini giving him a bottle of water, 'Here drink this.'

'Thanks', said Shiven accepting water and washing his face, 'I hate him because I know he has got you framed and won't rest until he has made you his girlfriend. You don't care a damn about him and he takes it as a greater challenge so that it fulfills his ego. I am telling you; you are slotted to be his next Kavya. I don't know if you can see it or not, but beware—he is there!'

Anuranjini looked at Shiven and shook her head, 'What rubbish are you saying? Are you out of your mind? How can you even think like that let alone speak it out?'

'I can', said Shiven, breathing easily, 'You have no idea what type of a weed he is. Now, you don't get offended but that is the truth. I hope and wish it more than anyone else on this earth that this won't happen. Remember, I will always be praying.'

Saying this Shiven grabbed his bag and walked away to his vehicle parked ahead. Anuranjini stared at the figure of Shiven walking away as she stood there holding her bag and bottle.

'Please don't go Shiven', said Anuranjini, painfully, 'I won't leave you. It is a promise. Please come back.'

Her computer chair bent a little back and she opened her eyes with a jolt. It was Monday and she was sitting in her cubicle at the office. She opened her eyes and saw Nimesh as usual hanging off her cubicle giving a look of utmost astonishment. He almost seemed scared.

'Is this a bad time?' asked Nimesh apprehensively.

'Yes it is', replied Anuranjini, appearing very tired suddenly, 'Do you want to ask anything?'

'No', said Nimesh, 'I have to call Vani; my fiancée. I will talk to you later.'

Nimesh scuttled away from her cubicle. Anuranjini rubbed her eyes and decided to get fresh and went over to the bathroom to wash her face.

Shiven always was right Anuranjini; she thought to herself; *It was you who was really slotted to be the troubled water and that is what your life is all about. Others must learn from your story. I seriously wish others do learn not to take idiotic decisions. You should be hung on the altar of intelligence so that even wise people don't make foolish mistakes—not at least of this much degree.*

She returned to her cubicle and continued to with her work. A deal was lying pending with a Canadian company and she had to close that by evening. If things worked out the way she had anticipated their company will be benefited by this deal. Just the terms and conditions had to be decided. She had already applied for three weeks' leave and since this one was a bit tough to manage, she had thought she will schedule it for later and get the deal sealed easily.

It won't work until you stop living in your head Anuranjini; the M.S.U days are so over. The romance, the songs, the promise of a bright future—is all finished. All that is left is this—You!

****

#7

The domestic airport at Vadodara has a homely appearance and it more or less gave a very "living-room" like feeling to anyone who got down there. Though it was not as huge as the Mumbai International Airport, it had all the amenities and conveniences of a domestic air terminus. Devashish Shastri had to deliver full one week seminar in the University auditorium in Vadodara and for that he had carried a briefcase full of lecture notes. As soon as he disembarked from the aircraft and walked towards the tarmac a huge gust of wind blew and lifted his hair. *It always is like this. This wind can knock a well built man down;* smiled Devashish.

'Had a very good stay somewhere?' asked a young boy, 'Anish. How are you?'

'Devashish Shastri', smiled back Devashish shaking hands with him, 'Just returning from Frankfurt. I had some research work going on since couple of years.'

'Oh the ivy league of extra ordinary men', smiled Anish back, 'And you are here for?'

'I have to deliver a week full of guest lectures', said Devashish smiling.

'Say at MSU?' asked Anish, 'I am a student there. I am returning after a week at Mumbai and my girlfriend has come to receive me. The staying away is all worth if the returning gives little pleasures.'

The door opened and they entered the arrival lounge. They both had to collect their luggage and the conveyer belt hadn't started yet.

'You seem to be a person of a higher stature', said Anish, smiling blissfully, 'Allow me to guess; you are not married.'

'Not married yet young man', said Devashish. He somehow liked this fellow very much. He was lively and very polite and had an aura of positive energy about him, 'This time when I will go home there are chances that I may have to look at a couple of parents' choices.'

Anish smiled back toothily.

'Which year are you in?' asked Devashish.

'Second year', replied Anish, 'Mathematics.'

Devashish nodded at him. Their luggage arrived and both grabbed their bags and started to walk. Just as they crossed the threshold of the exit a girl squealed and came running towards them.

'Vedika', said Anish, 'And he is Mr. Devashish Shastri. We'll soon find him at our college. He is coming to deliver guest lectures.'

'A pleasure to meet you sir', said the girl respectfully shaking hands with him.

Devashish smiled at them and saying a good bye went to find a taxi. As he sat in the taxi, he simply said a silent prayer for them wishing nothing ever wrong happened between them. He liked them both. They appeared quite like a "made for each other" pair.

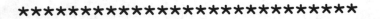

****

#8

'Miss Anuranjini Roy', addressed the team leader at the team meeting in the conference room, 'I really wish to congratulate you as the deal with the Canadian company has been neatly closed and all the terms and conditions are appropriately agreed upon. This will lead to a performance appraisal. Everyone; please give a big hand to Miss Roy.'

Anuranjini smiled back as everyone gave a huge applause.

'Also Miss Roy', said the team leader, 'You wanted a three week leave for medical purpose and that has been granted. You can really take a break and recover yourselves fully.'

'Thank you', said Anuranjini smiling faintly, 'This will really mean a lot to me.'

'The meeting just ended', said the team leader.

All the team members came out praising Anuranjini. That deal had been pending since last two weeks and nobody had that much guts to take it up. Anuranjini felt that she had lost a lot of things and this task might just enhance her confidence. Though the seniors had refused and had advised her not to play with fire—the lately suicidal approach of Anuranjini was only encouraging her. So she decided to take up the deal and had been studying it since many nights; sleepless as she always was.

She returned to her cubicle and started picking up a lot of things that she had to carry with herself.

'Can I help Anuranjini?' asked Nimesh.

'No thanks', said Anuranjini putting a lot of papers on the table, 'I can manage.'

An envelope fell from the table and Nimesh bent to pick it up. It was addressed from the Vadodara Domestic Court and Nimesh's mouth fell open. This contained Anuranjini's divorce papers. Anuranjini glanced at it.

'Lo', she said wearily yet smiling, 'You got it. Have a look at it if your curiosity is getting the better of you.'

Nimesh opened the envelope and glanced at the contents inside it. He felt as if the page stank with Rishabh's malice and he suddenly felt a wave of nausea. He folded the papers and put it inside the envelope and exited for a cup of coffee.

Anuranjini smiled at Nimesh's leaving figure. She knew how he felt. That is how even she had felt when for the first time the papers had been delivered to her. But she had fought it out all on her own. When she felt her ship was going to sink soon, she had consulted a therapist and tried working out a routine. Even that didn't seem to be helping but while talking with the therapist she could put her inhibitions to rest.

Now she felt she was more at peace than she was more than a year back when all hell had broken loose.

Next Monday I'll be a spinster again; thought Anuranjini scornfully smiling to herself, *I will party! Hoot! Hoot!*

****

#9

The Café Coffee Day, next to Pride Hotel, in Ahmadabad is home for all type of people. The college going crowd and many office goers find the place a haven for cozy chats—indeed a lot could happen over a coffee and the Café was a personal favorite to the majority population.

Rishabh was seated there with Madhvi and the atmosphere between them was not ambient. Madhvi was not in a very good mood and Rishabh was staring at his cup and not looking up. Madhvi too, was twiddling her fingers on the rim of the cup of her coffee.

'Look', said Rishabh breaking the long silence, 'This has got to work Madhvi. You have got to help me in working it. The marriage I had was an idiotic decision I had taken and I accept that it was my entire mistake and so I am trying to rectify that blunder. I was young, energetic, foolish and possibly never serious. I need your help. Without your help I cannot do it.'

'What if you say after some years that the marriage with me too was a blunder and that again you want to rectify it?' asked Madhvi, scornfully, 'I will be the laughing stock; the second Anuranjini of your life—not to mention that my life will be ruined.'

'No Madhvi', said Rishabh taking her hands in his, 'That was a time when I was in college and the superstar. I hardly used brains then because I had many others using their brains for me. When I told mom and dad then that Anuranjini was my choice and they saw her photos; they were really impressed. Nothing else mattered then and so it doesn't today. But the person does matter Madhvi and I know it is you. Why do you think then in six years of relationship nothing like even a spark happened between us? We don't share anything in common at all. Though we are married, we are still strangers looking at each other. Anything that is wrong is always rectified by god even if man takes time in realizing it. I want you to understand it the same way.'

Madhvi looked at him but still she didn't seem convinced. That feeling gave away on her face and she asked,

'Anuranjini is still a part of you Rishabh; accept it or not', she replied, 'When she said a small thing that day in Mc Donald's you got immediately flared up. She knows you well and those chords that strike you off your mark. Believe me Rishabh, even if you are going to get divorced in a week's time; you will never be able to divorce her off your mind and soul. She is that much a part of you. These days while addressing me; you call me Anuranjini instead of Madhvi. You are not able to banish her from yourself. A relation of six years is not easy to forget.'

'Exactly', said Rishabh clasping Madhvi's hands tightly and smiling, 'So will you please help me get her out of my system? I want to spend the next better half of my life with you Madhvi and that is not a lie.'

Madhvi was not sure whether she wanted to really believe the person sitting opposite to her. Yet, he was so handsome and appeared quite truthful that she didn't feel like wanting to deny him and then again, she remembered Anuranjini's condition; quite bedraggled and the look of a person who had lost a lot of weight and peace of mind in quite short a time. Anuranjini's condition had frozen all nerves in her and for the first time in three months of her relationship with Rishabh; Madhvi had felt actually scared of the fellow with whom she had been going out. There was an unsaid fear in her that told her that Rishabh was not a very good guy and that if she was not careful; very soon she and Anuranjini may resemble like sisters.

Let us hope Rishabh is the fellow of your life; thought Madhvi; *At least he has not done any damage in your life so far.*

★★★★★★★★★★★★★★★★★★★★★★★★

#10

Anuranjini was preparing a cup of coffee and the television in her flat too was on. She really believed in keeping herself updated on the day to day news. *Some day the news comes handy;* she remembered her former Team Leader's words. Generally too, Anuranjini believed in keeping herself intact with the latest happenings on earth; a habit that had been inculcated in the family by her parents.

Her phone went off. It was her elder brother.

'Hello', she spoke into the phone. Her throat seemed to have gone hoarse and her voice was low.

'How are you doing Andy?' asked Shantanu, her elder brother, 'When are you coming home?'

'I am okay Dada', replied Anuranjini, 'Mostly I will come on Saturday evening. I really am not in a very good shape to make an appearance at the doorstep. Mom and dad will be scared by my condition.'

'Andy', said Shantanu, 'I want you to be happy and in good shape before you appear in the court for gods' sake! Rishabh will be there all gloating and celebrating his victory. I want you too, to be in the same euphoria.'

'Dada I am always in some euphoria, am I not?' said Anuranjini wearily, her throat heavy as tears slowly started, 'That lead me to some trouble, hasn't it? I will be fine. I have full confidence that after Monday I will be in a much better shape. The black phase of my life that I thought would never end is finally ending and I cannot more than thank god for the good he does to me. He always rescues me at the right time.'

Shantanu gave a wan smile to himself. His sister always was like that; even if anyone did something wrong or bad to her, she could not retaliate. She had never learnt that and that was the reason why he was always so protective about her. While at school too many of the fellow students always found it easy to manipulate Anuranjini. It was easy to make a fool of her and she still would never react except for the fact that at night she would endlessly cry and then relate the incident to her brother and the next day he had to fight all the goons away.

Then, Shiven entered into her life. Both were very good students right from the very first day of their college. They were the teachers' favorites and other students always asked doubts to them which they were only too glad to help. How much ever they scored or won laurels in competitions, they never were the attention seekers and yet staying with Shiven; Anuranjini had learnt to fight it tough. Shantanu was actually very happy that Shiven was her friend. Shiven and Shantanu got along a lot because their thinking was of the same frequency. Shantanu trusted Shiven a lot and secretly he had even wished that Shiven and Anuranjini should fall in love with each other. He knew that even if their parents denied, Shiven was a person whom no parent on earth could deny.

'Andy', said Shantanu, 'Do come on Friday, will you? I want to spend some time with the Andy I knew. Let us see if we are the same brother-sister we always were. Even if anything out in the world goes bad, things between both of us don't change. Supriya also wants you at home. She has been really tensed about you. Your divorce is affecting her too and she wants to know that you are in good condition.'

Anuranjini burst into tears. She seemed to have forgotten what soft words are. Ever since Rishabh had changed his track, it had been abusive language and wordy duel at home. She never really wanted the matter to go public. She could willingly have suffered her entire life too hadn't Rishabh demanded a divorce. She was ready to compromise everything in her life to make the marriage work. Before Rishabh's declaration for divorce, she used to visit her parents every fifteen days but now it had been a year since she had come home though Ahmedabad and Vadodara were not at great distances.

Supriya, Shantanu's wife, too had been equally tensed. Shantanu knew both were talking about the day to day fights going on at the Joshi household. Supriya gave a very patient ear and came with new solutions to a never ending series of problems. Shantanu loved her for this. Other than him and his parents, it was Supriya who was bravely supporting her. All the while she was hearing to Anuranjini's daily cries, not once had she mentioned anything about divorcing. She too wanted this marriage to work as much as Anuranjini.

'Yes dada', replied Anuranjini wiping her tears, 'I will be there on Friday evening. I will talk to you later. Bye.'

She disconnected the line and went and washed her face. She looked at herself in the mirror and found that she now nowhere resembled that college beauty she was six years ago. Not only was she six years older she seemed to have outgrown her age in last one year—she resembled somewhere between thirty and forty.

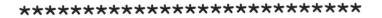

The Maharaja Sayajirao University has a huge campus; almost like a campus that one reads in some book or gets to see in a typical Hindi movie. It has an assortment of gates of which all are functional. The gate that led to the front of the Science Departments wound its way out and joined the Sayajigunj road. The Sayajigunj road is always thronged with huge crowds as it is one of the mainstream roads. It connects the old city to the main city. Also it is near to the famous Kamati baug, the planetarium and the museum.

'Shiven, will you please drive slowly? I am getting scared', almost shouted Anuranjini over the roar of wind, 'Can't you see the whole damn crowd?'

'I can and you shut up!' yelled Shiven.

With a swipe, he cut through the crowd and took a turn and entered the campus through the gate. As soon as he neared the parking in front of the department, he applied the brakes and Anuranjini skidded and almost fell on top of him.

'Everyday, this is the same story', said Anuranjini scowling as she got down and tried to make her hair behave, 'My whole hair is a mess!'

'This is better than your silly two wheeler', he replied setting his hair looking into his rear-view, 'I feel ashamed driving it.'

'Why don't you let me drive my vehicle then?' scowled Anuranjini.

'Hold and behold!' said Shiven, 'I will never sit behind a girl.'

'Unnecessarily chauvinistic!' remarked Anuranjini, 'Nobody will make fun of you for that. All the misconceptions you boys have; I really get irritated.'

'Come on, now stop grumbling', said Shiven smiling at her indignant face and grabbing her shoulders and pushing her, 'We have got very good lectures today. Hurry up.'

'Is there a place for me in this lecture?' said Rishabh joining them. Rishabh came walking from behind and joined the duo, walking on the other side of Anuranjini. He had not forgotten the duel with Shiven.

Shiven got infuriated, 'I will catch you later Andy. I have got work.'

And without any word, he left the two. Anuranjini got scared when Shiven left. Rishabh heaved a sigh of relief.

'Good Riddance!' said Rishabh smiling, 'So how are you today my beauty?'

'Not so good', scowled Anuranjini, 'Why the hell do you have to show your face so early in the morning? Shiven got angry because of you.'

'I came to meet you', said Rishabh surprised, 'I thought you would appreciate it and not shout at me. Shiven is so important in your life that even my company for five minutes is not permitted, is that so?'

'Yes it is', replied Anuranjini gritting her teeth, 'Shiven is a very important person in my life. He knows me very well and I don't risk anything for him.'

'And what about me?' asked Rishabh looking into her eyes, 'I know my impression is not so good but won't you have even little time for me? I know Shiven is a very important person for you but even I am your classmate. It won't hurt if you spend some time with a fellow classmate, will it?'

Anuranjini stared at him and saw the look of innocence in his eyes. The look shook her heart and she felt sorry for him.

'I will some other time', said Anuranjini, 'Right now we have got lectures and I want to attend it.'

Saying Anuranjini left him and walked away at top speed. She joined Shiven at her seat beside him.

'How was the date?' he scowled as he opened the book and ferociously turned the page.

'It was not a date', replied Anuranjini scowling at him, 'Do you mind not jibing me for his idiocy?'

The lecture started and the professor entered. The lecture was really very interesting and Shiven *enjoyed the most. He liked this particular subject a lot; Heat and Thermodynamics. When the lecture ended, their attendance was taken.*

'Anuranjini Roy', called out their professor.

Anuranjini for the first time in her three years in Physics had not paid attention to her attendance call. When she hadn't answered, their professor was forced to call her name out. Yet she didn't answer. Shiven shook her and brought her out of her reverie.

'Yes sir. I am present', she answered.

'Anuranjini, aren't you in mood today?' said their professor with a mild crease on his forehead. He proceeded with the attendance.

'What is wrong with you Andy?' asked Shiven, patting her mildly. More shock awaited him as he saw that Anuranjini hadn't written down any notes of the lectures and instead in a very flowery pattern written the word 'Rishabh'. Shiven was so angry that he left the lecture hall without a word to Anuranjini. Anuranjini realizing that Shiven had left at top disgusted speed quickly tore the page off her book and crumpled it and threw it on the ground.

She exited the lecture hall but could not find Shiven anywhere in the whole distance.

There in the classroom, Rishabh came down to where Anuranjini had thrown the paper, picked it and read it. He felt completely satisfied and smiling to himself, exited for the canteen pocketing the paper.

Anuranjini tried to get Shiven on the phone but he was not picking it up. The ring went on continuously and then Anuranjini broke out of her vision.

The phone as well as the doorbell was ringing simultaneously. She realized that she still was in the bathroom and the phone was on the broad wash basin. She quickly exited the bathroom wiping her face on the clean bathroom towel.

She opened the door and there stood Nimesh with his fiancée Vani.

'I just came to give you an invitation for a party tomorrow at my place', said Nimesh looking utterly scared, 'I hope I didn't seriously disturb you in your work.'

'No, not at all' smiled back Anuranjini. The tear stains were still visible on her face, 'Please do come in.'

'Oh no thank you', said Nimesh politely, 'We have more invitations to give. I will really catch up with you on some other day.'

'Okay as you wish', replied Anuranjini still keeping a fake smile on, 'Take care and thanks. I will be there. Bye.'

The two smiled and left as Anuranjini closed the door of her flat.

Outside Vani asked Nimesh, 'Something is not okay with her. What is it?'

'Better not ask', muttered Nimesh as they got into the lift and descended. He knew very well that Anuranjini had cried and that she was alone in the flat. He felt scared for her but he also felt helpless at the situation.

★★★★★★★★★★★★★★★★★★★★★★★★

#11

Devashish Shastri told the taxi driver to take him on a tour of the city. The very first step in the city had been nice and though it was dark already, he was not in a mood to head straight for home.

'What happened sir?' asked the driver looking into the rear view, 'Don't you want to go home?'

'No', replied Devashish Shastri smiling, 'I like your city very much. It is worth more than a ride.'

'That is true sir', said the driver, 'What do you do?'

'I am a junior researcher and I don't work here', said Devashish, leaning back and resting 'I just came from Germany. Nothing invigorates me as good as a good evening ride though. There I used to remain more than twenty hours inside my room with my fellow research mates and get serious headaches. Now I am free for two months and am in a jolly good mood.'

'Wow', said the taxi driver though he didn't exactly know what research was or the subject of Devashish's interest, 'You are a brilliant fellow sir.

It is not every day that I get to meet such smart people.'

'Thank you buddy', smiled back Devashish, 'Thanks a lot.'

The city was very fresh—windy and cool. The streets were full with evening traffic and the orange street lights glared from great heights. The dust hadn't settled though and people on two wheelers could be occasionally seen wiping their eyes. The old city area was deserted and people seemed to have retreated into their homes while Alkapuri area just seemed to be waking up and glittering golden.

When finally Devashish's ride ended he asked the driver to turn it towards his home. The driver had kept some good music and both went flying towards Devashish's destination. When he arrived at the gate there waited his mother and his younger sister, Malvika, his elder brother Dhyanesh, his sister-in-law and his dad; all teary eyed and excited at his arrival.

'How much?' asked Devashish to the driver.

'I am not sure how much should I charge— anything that you feel right', replied the driver humbly.

'Well', said Devashish nodding, 'In that case I suggest you take this thousand rupees note. It simplifies all calculations.' Saying Devashish began to unload his bags from the cab. The driver ran forward and helped him. Giving a last wave to Devashish, the driver pulled his cab out.

'Devu', said Mrs. Shastri, 'I thought you were never coming. What took you so long?'

'Mom', said Devashish smiling, 'I had gone for a drive.'

Mrs. Shastri came forward and lunged on her son and hugged him tight, weeping into his shoulder.

'I won't let you go Devu', she sobbed, 'I won't ever let you go. No need to do research. We have got enough money in the family. No need to do any work out of the country.'

'Ma', smiled Devashish at his mother's tears, 'Mom please stop crying. Is that how you welcome your son?'

Mrs. Shastri let him off. His elder brother came forward and helped him carry the luggage inside. The atmosphere inside the Shastri household was that of rejoicing. A bucket of lukewarm water awaited him and then a variety of dishes. His clothes were ready that were of pure cotton and quite fluffy. His room was just the way he wanted. After dinner, the family settled down to chat with him.

'Do you know something Devu?' said Dhyanesh smiling, passing him an ice-cream cup, 'In short time, we may have to visit some homes. We are planning your marriage now that you are free for two months; if not a marriage then an engagement at the very least.'

'Why so early?' exclaimed Devashish with a quizzical expression.

'It is too late', replied Mrs. Shastri, 'I doubt one of them is even a second marriage. At your age, it is difficult to get single women. Mostly everyone gets married early.'

'Come on mom', said Devashish, 'I cannot afford to get married now. You know my work is demanding. After two months I have to report at Dehradun and probably after that I will leave for Germany. I don't have time and space to maintain a family right now.'

'Now don't act Mr. Busy with me alright?' said Mrs. Shastri, giving a second helping to Malvika, 'Many scientists get married. How is that they are able to maintain a family life? Next Thursday or Friday we have to go to see a girl. Her name is Meera. Let us see if you like her or not.'

'Did you say there is a second marriage case?' asked Devashish.

'Yes. I think so', replied Mr. Shastri, Devashish's father, 'The girl is good. We haven't seen her picture or we hardly know her name; but the pundit said she belongs to a good family. Are you interested in marrying her?'

'I don't think that we will want a woman who is marrying a second time', said Mrs. Shastri, 'We still have better options. We don't know why it's the second marriage but we are not interested—no need to inquire much.'

Devashish shook his head. His mom was very concerned about him and his life ahead. Ever since he had gone to Dehradun he hadn't even breathed a word about a girl. In college, he used to have very limited number of female friends. But the seriousness of the work had rendered the flavor and essence of youth quite useless in him. He felt that all this was nonsense and he didn't consider marriage at all on charts.

'Meera', he remarked, 'Name is good.'

'So is the girl', said Mrs. Shastri smiling, 'You will like her I am quite sure.'

Devashish smiled to himself. *I may get a bride after all*, said Devashish to himself, *And then who knows? You may really want to settle down in Germany with her. Life has just started in the real meaning.*

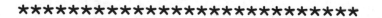

#12

Nimesh knows how to organize a party after all, thought Anuranjini to herself. She was at Nimesh's place. It was the next day and Nimesh and Vani had hosted the party well enough. All the office mates along with close friends had been invited. There was food, music and soft dancing going on. Anuranjini was standing alone in a corner with a glass of juice in her hand.

A young man of about say twenty eight or so came over to her,

'Nice party, right?'

Anuranjini turned to him. Though she didn't speak to absolute strangers, she assumed he had to be Nimesh's friend, 'Yeah. Thank god I didn't have to organize this. His last one had been a serious headache and by the end of it all, it had truly affected my nerves.'

The young fellow laughed and gave his hand, 'Vishwas.'

'Anuranjini', she replied taking his hand. She was not sure if she should have, but nevertheless she gave a smile.

'Anuranjini, I know you well', said Vishwas, 'You are Rishabh's wife, aren't you? Rishabh is my best pal.'

The color drained from her face at the mention of Rishabh and she once again seemed to be bedraggled.

'Please don't mind', said Vishwas, immediately noticing the change in her face, 'I don't want you to judge me because of Rishabh.'

Anuranjini regained her composure, 'No. I seriously don't judge others by him.'

Anuranjini didn't say anything further and watched on as few of Nimesh's friends danced. The air between she and Vishwas was stiff and there was an obvious irritation written on her face.

'I know', said Vishwas, breaking the silence finally, 'That you don't have a reason to trust me either. But let me tell you one thing if that makes you feel better; what Rishabh did was hundred percent wrong. He didn't have a right whatsoever to spoil your life.'

Anuranjini didn't utter a word and stared at him.

'He introduced me to Madhvi', he continued.

'Her name is Madhvi?' asked Anuranjini cutting him.

'Yes', he replied, 'Both work in different companies and their offices are on different floors. They come to the parking together. Lunch break times are same. That is how they used to meet. Rishabh is a flying bee. He is the first person who gets the news when a . . .'

'. . . new flower blooms', finished Anuranjini smiling, 'That is what happened with me too. That is what the whole world calls him. In graduation, he had made me feel very special. I thought he was just flirting. But when his parents came home and claimed that they wanted me as the bride for their son, I felt for the first time that may be somebody can like me too, may be Rishabh was after all changing for the better. Every boy has this nature—after all it is college. Many mature up over the years, Rishabh didn't. He is no more twenty, but he still behaves like one.'

'He told me you had an affair with your best friend Shiven', said Vishwas very carefully. He somehow liked Anuranjini very much and didn't wish to hurt her delicacy.

'A theory that he has been singing out to anyone who listens to him', laughed Anuranjini scornfully, 'I haven't spoken to Shiven since last six years. The last time I had met him was when he had come home to give me my wedding present. He didn't even come for my marriage. He got so much aggravated at my decision that he changed his number and lost contact with me. I don't deny his anger. Three continuous days he had tried dissuading me from saying yes to Rishabh's proposal. But I was such an idiot at that time that I didn't pay attention to him. Consequences I hardly wish to explicit.'

'He is the biggest . . .'

'. . . please don't call Rishabh any names', interrupted Anuranjini, 'Shiven himself had told me that if I said yes to Rishabh and got married to him, we would have to stop talking with each other because it doesn't appear nice if I, being married, chatted with him the whole day like college friends.

What I believe is that he used this reason as an excuse to say goodbye forever. Even I agree that after marriage status of every relation changes. But I had not expected Shiven to cut off completely from me. I believe this is how it was meant for me—no best friend and no husband.' She gave a sad, wan smile.

'I really feel sorry for you Anuranjini', said Vishwas, 'I am quite sure Rishabh doesn't deserve a great human being like you to be his wife and I wish I could salute Shiven.'

'Thanks', smiled Anuranjini, 'You are one of those few people on Rishabh's side who isn't giving me a judgmental stare. Many of his friends think I was responsible for this divorce. Thanks a lot.'

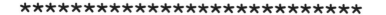

****

#13

'Why the heck aren't you picking my phone?' shouted Anuranjini when finally Shiven lifted her call.

'Because I don't want to talk to you!' yelled back Shiven.

'What big a crime have I done?' shouted Anuranjini again.

'No you haven't', said Shiven in the same tone, 'I was an idiot trying to explain you why that Rishabh should be avoided.'

'Then you are an idiot!' screamed Anuranjini.

'Not as big as you though!' continued Shiven, his voice exceeding the conventional seventy decibel deadline after which he threw the phone on his bed, switching it off.

Anuranjini was taken aback and she got even angrier. Without a second thought, she exited her home on top speed. Her mother was scared when she heard Anuranjini yelling like that in her room. Shantanu too had heard her and was wondering what had happened to make her scream like that.

She jumped on her vehicle and vroomed all her way to Shiven's residence. When she reached there, his mother was out watering plants.

'Hello girl, how are you?' she asked pleasantly.

'I am fine auntie thank you', she replied smiling, 'Is Shiven in here?'

'Yeah, Go right in. He was shouting at someone; god knows who. You may be able to soothe him', she said.

'Of course', said Anuranjini, 'He was shouting at me.'

Shiven's mother was flabbergasted. Why was Shiven shouting on Anuranjini? thought Shiven's mother.

Anuranjini entered Shiven's room with a blast and she stood at the doorway, her face contorted in a fury like that of black thunder.

'What is your problem Mr. Shiven?' she said acidly.

'You', he turned with lightning in his eyes, 'You are such a dunce that I am sick and tired of explaining it to you that Rishabh is not going to let you in peace.'

'He didn't say he is in love with me or the usual rubbish', said Anuranjini still angry, 'He said he just wanted to spend some time and that doesn't mean he is all head over heels.'

'Oh wow! Miss Beauty without Brains!' again rose Shiven's voice, 'Spending some time with him, are you? That is where it all begins. I really wouldn't have bothered if you befriended any other

fellow on earth but Rishabh! You know him very well and yet you are fraternizing with him!'

'Exactly when did I fraternize?' said Anuranjini rising like a sleeping python.

'You don't have to', replied Shiven scornfully, 'For the first time in so many years, you didn't take down notes and scribbled his name in a flowery pattern. This is a vicious cycle and Miss Anuranjini you are in it. It is easy for anyone to sweep you off your feet, isn't it?'

Anuranjini froze and her anger ebbed away. Shiven too cooled down and had a drink from the bottle lying on his study table.

'We compare the notes and make a final writing in the notebook and discuss in the library', said Shiven in a hurt tone, 'We had no notes to compare today in three years Andy. Nothing can hurt me more than that. I thought we both cherished Physics and we like the subject. Somehow, Rishabh managed to overpower your interest for Physics too.'

Anuranjini didn't speak anything but only blinked back at Shiven.

'Andy', he said, clutching on to his bottle, 'If you too have developed a liking for Rishabh then I promise I will respect your decision. I am your friend and whatever be your happiness will be my happiness. But it will be my duty to advise you to stay out of troubled waters Andy and I will continue to do so till I know that you can keep your head above the water. When I realize the ship is going to sink, I will stop advising you.'

There were tears in Anuranjini's eyes. She realized that Shiven feared of losing her friendship. Though Shiven was the college favorite and had many friends, he had only one very good friend and that was Anuranjini.

Without another word Anuranjini left from Shiven's room. She didn't even stop to chat with his mother and saying a polite bye left his home.

I hope Shiven doesn't get insecure; thought Anuranjini. The wind was flying in her face as she drove and then she opened her eyes.

She was seated in her balcony and looking out at the streets of Ahmadabad where the traffic was rolling away in flashes of light. *God, why can't there be a time machine? she thought; I want to rectify a big mistake. God! Why did I leave Physics?*

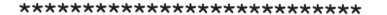

✹✹✹✹✹✹✹✹✹✹✹✹✹✹✹✹✹✹✹✹✹✹✹✹✹

#14

The doorbell rang and Rishabh went to answer it. Vishwas was standing there with some food and drinks.

'Hi', said Vishwas. It was not the usual peppy "hi" but Rishabh was busy staring at the food.

'Hello Buddy', said Rishabh, 'Nice that you came along. I need to talk about something important to you.'

'So do I', said Vishwas keeping the food on the coffee table.

Vishwas went to the wash basin to wash his face. He could not remove Anuranjini's image from his head. Her grace, charm and grandeur and yet her tired look when he had taken Rishabh's name. He wanted to save Rishabh's marriage; had he been in Rishabh's place he wouldn't have let Anuranjini leave him for anyone on this planet. He wistfully wished he had met Anuranjini before Rishabh.

They both settled down in the sofa as Rishabh started a movie DVD.

'Let me start first', said Rishabh happily, 'After the divorce the very next week, I and Madhvi are marrying. Actually not so grandly, just a private party with the official papers being signed. Then next month, we are going off to Madhvi's ancestral home in Darjeeling and marrying there in a grand procession. But officially, next week I am getting married to her. How do you like my plan?'

'Wow', said Vishwas uninterestedly, 'Grand plans really eh?'

'Yes', said Rishabh gleefully, 'You are going to be my best man buddy. Though we don't have that system, but you have to host the marriage party.'

Vishwas said venomously, 'What if I say I don't want to?'

'What do you mean Vishwas?' said Rishabh taken aback.

'I had gone to Nimesh's party yesterday', said Vishwas in the same acid tone.

'Your school friend, right?' said Rishabh.

'Yes', continued Vishwas in the same poison, 'I had met Anuranjini there. Rishabh, for no human being on earth I would have been the best man except you had you been marrying not spoiling her life. Have you taken a look at her? She is all devastated and shattered and you are making plans and organizing stuff for your second wedding? You don't have an idea that she is a gem of a person and you are all set to kill her slowly.'

'Dude', said Rishabh seriously, 'Take it easy. She still is my wife and I don't take good words about her from another man; even if he is my best friend.'

'I wouldn't utter a word about her if the situations were different', said Vishwas giving a disbelieving look at him, 'But you are the limit Rishabh. I was just about to say a swear word to you and she stopped me. She is still all ready to give this marriage one more trial but you broke off the marriage in your mind a long time back. What in the wide world are you planning to do in future? Act like an Indian Casanova? Rishabh please give it a second thought before you go for the divorce. You can still call off the proceedings. Had I been in your place I wouldn't have let her go.'

'Oh yeah?' said Rishabh maliciously, 'Then don't let her go Vishwas. She is all free from next week and stays two blocks off the Radio station. Don't give me advice on how to deal with my family life. You be concerned with yours.'

'Yes', said Vishwas getting up, 'I thought about that sometime back; thinking what a big, pathetic and disgusting person you are. I am wondering that inauspicious time when I befriended you and thought you were my best pal. You just like to use human beings according to your will and that is the only thing that you are good at. Mr. Rishabh Joshi, I think we are through with our so many years of friendship forever. You will never find me anywhere near you after today. I swear.'

Rishabh stood there completely shell-shocked. He didn't utter a word but then recovered almost immediately. Vishwas walked away, opened the door and wore his shoes.

'I will still send you an invitation card', called back Rishabh as Vishwas exited from the front door.

'And I will still send you a gift', replied Vishwas turning. He waved and then went down the stairs taking two steps at a time. He really wanted to get away from Rishabh's atmosphere.

There are better people surviving on earth; said Vishwas to himself.

Anuranjini was trying to go to sleep but some visuals of Shiven and Rishabh were constantly mixing in her head. She tried to shake off the images but again they seem to be getting heavier. She glanced at her watch; it was just 9:00 pm. She had skipped her dinner. After previous day's party she seemed to have altogether lost appetite and couldn't make the food to work in her system. Whole day she had been inside her flat and had gone out in the evening only to pick some vegetables and get milk and take a casual walk in the park. She had thought she would watch a movie in her home and had even bought a DVD but she didn't feel like watching it. After somehow managing to struggle through a cup of coffee, she had decided to retire for the day but again; she was unable to sleep.

The doorbell rang and she got startled. *Who is visiting at 9.00 in the evening?* thought Anuranjini. She threw back the cover and ran down to the main door.

'Who is it?' called Anuranjini. She had stopped trusting the human race—specifically the men.

'Open up. It is your husband', said the voice in a drawl.

Anuranjini froze but nevertheless opened up the door. There stood Rishabh at the doorway. He was smiling very evilly and pushed his way in.

'What do you want now?' said Anuranjini alarmed and confused.

'Definitely not you', said Rishabh looking at her coldly. The reply stung Anuranjini badly, 'But I need to ask you something. What the hell did you pout to Vishwas that he broke up his friendship with me?'

'Just the truth', replied Anuranjini impassively, 'He asked some questions to which I supplied accurate answers. He has a right to know the truth you know; he is your *best* pal.'

Rishabh's eyes narrowed, 'Listen young woman, I don't want that rubbish from you ever again. If you go announcing around the globe that I did something bad to you and your life spoiled; well so far I have been considerably decent. I don't want to really spoil your life.'

'You already have Rishabh', said Anuranjini laughing scornfully, 'How much more damage can you do? At the most kill me? Well, one needs to have guts for that and that I know, you don't have. Just go away. Anyway, I hadn't gone asking in the crowd who is Rishabh's friend. He had come to talk to me.'

'Whatever be the reason, I am not concerned. But my friends or foes, you won't open your mouth even at gun-point', said Rishabh threateningly.

'After Monday, the wish will all be mine Rish', said Anuranjini venomously.

'Exactly', said a voice from the doorway. It was Vishwas.

'You aren't a man Rishabh', he said coming inside, 'I knew you would come here to confront her that is why I took her address from Nimesh and decided to pay a visit. It paid off. Threatening a poor, broken-hearted woman, are you? What sort of an imbecile are you Rishabh; the one that cannot be categorized?'

Anuranjini looked frightfully at both. Instantly she was reminded of the fight between Shiven and Rishabh. She didn't want that happening.

'Please don't fight over me', said Anuranjini intervening, 'Act sensibly guys, please don't fight.'

Rishabh chuckled cruelly, 'Last time, her best friend had fought with me, hadn't he? Where is he to save you today? Punch a hole in me and remove my eyes? Wait! Do I see *my* best friend now?'

Anuranjini choked hearing Rishabh mimic Shiven. She had never expected Shiven to be mentioned—least of all from Rishabh.

'Please go both of you', said Anuranjini. Vishwas and Rishabh were looking at each other daggers.

Rishabh left scornfully. Vishwas just stared at him until he was out of sight. He then turned to her,

'My sister Shweta is coming over', he said, 'I don't trust Rishabh. We both will stay with you till you leave for Vadodara. I hope you don't mind.'

Anuranjini smiled back, 'Thanks a lot Vishwas. I am highly grateful to you.'

Within the hour, Shweta had arrived. Vishwas's sister Shweta was a real company when she came. Though smaller than Vishwas, she was tons and tons of fun and within half an hour the entire atmosphere was rent with positive energy, giggles and enthusiasm. Anuranjini was really shell-shocked to see a person of such puzzling energy flying around. The DVD player was going on in full volume and Shweta was singing along with the song.

'She is like that, a bit weird', said Vishwas suddenly going red, 'I hope she doesn't embarrass me.'

'She is great Vishwas', said Anuranjini smiling, 'Nobody can tell she is in her final year graduation; so independent and such a pleasantly noisy kid.'

'I am scared', said Vishwas apprehensively, 'She likes to break crockery and is very bad at handling things. She generally too is bad at handling things—especially tangible ones. I think we both will have to be damn careful with giving her breakable stuffs. She is a ranker but can't do one thing otherwise—not at all good at household stuffs.'

'What is she planning next?' asked Anuranjini as she helped Vishwas get things settled.

'MBA', said Vishwas, handing over some packets, 'She is a great talker. She can sell snow to a polar bear. That is what her plan is; MBA in marketing. God! Her customers *will have to* buy just so that she stops her jabber.'

'Don't say like that', said Anuranjini bursting into laughter, 'She is really fantastic. I am sure nobody around her can afford to shed even a tear.'

'Yeah', said Vishwas, 'That is true. The secret I believe is that she is not into silly *boyfriend-ish* stuff. She has got a gang of some ten friends—all studious lot. They enjoy studying and hang around together. If you have a good group, you don't need one special person in your life.'

Anuranjini felt someone had punched something into her tummy and she felt the oxygen choke in her throat. She had a glass of water.

'What shall we eat?' screamed Shweta from the kitchen.

Vishwas ran and skidded to a halt in the kitchen, 'No. Shweta don't touch . . . you will drop . . .'

There was a tinkle, a thud and a crash as two melamine plates came crashing down on the kitchen floor. Anuranjini ran and stood at the doorway, took a look and burst into laughter. Shweta was standing no doubt; but Vishwas was on the floor and the two plates had crashed around his feet. More funny was the expression of anger and disbelief that was written on Vishwas's face.

'I will clear up', said Anuranjini coming forward.

Shweta ran out of the kitchen and Vishwas ran after her, calling out names and trying to grab her hair so that he could hit her.

'Never challenge a black belt', teased Shweta as she dodged and laughed at him. Vishwas was panting and puffing and had stopped to grab a breath.

Anuranjini was watching the episode with highest interest. *Oh God! Happiness of this type does exist. I had totally forgotten that there is something like happiness and laughter.*

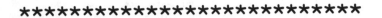

#15

Devashish Shastri liked the campus of the University and felt quite at home. It was as if the campus had come out of a story book or was the set of a movie. Students; some in groups and some in couples were all around and there were teachers taking a walk, switching between various department buildings. He had to go to the Department of Physics where he was to deliver his guest lecture.

'Mr. Shastri', greeted the head of the department, 'The pleasure will be all ours.'

'Good morning sir', greeted Devashish, 'Have all the students escaped?'

'Actually no', said the head, chuckling appreciatively, 'Many students from other departments too insisted on joining the physics students. There is a large crowd.'

'I was expecting a gang of maximum ten students', replied Devashish, 'I've lost habit of being in crowd after Frankfurt. I hope this isn't going to be a difficult first session.'

The head laughed, 'No. The students want to really hear you speak.'

Devashish was wondering; *There seems to be a larger crowd of career savvy kids*. He sat chatting with the head for some more time.

'I take your leave sir', said Devashish, standing up and shaking hands with him, 'I will now proceed towards the class.'

The head shook hands with him and Devashish left. While walking towards the classroom he met up with a familiar character.

'Good morning sir. I am Anish. Remember?' said the young fellow.

'Of course I do', replied Devashish, 'Mathematics, right?'

'Ditto', said Anish smiling, 'I suppose you will have lots to share regarding your research with us.'

'Yeah, I do', said Devashish. Talking with him reminded him of his own days when he too was young, energetic and study—monger, 'I hope I won't lull you into slumber.'

'No, you won't', he replied, 'I attend all guest lecturers; sometimes in other departments too because if I believe it is informative, I don't miss a chance. My friends make fun of me that I am being just too paranoid about studies. But frankly speaking, when we have intellectual discussions, I dominate because of all the extra information; all thanks to visiting faculties like you.'

'Don't you ever freak out or whatever your age group calls it?' asked Devashish.

'Oh yeah I do', replied Anish brightly, 'I go for a movie every weekend and occasionally with parents too but I study also.'

Devashish really wished he had a younger brother like Anish. The fellow was like a packet of energy and yet he studied and enjoyed. He seemed like the perfect son, student, friend and boyfriend. If the crop that had turned up to listen to him were like Anish, he was sure he was going to enjoy sharing his knowledge with them.

The type of students change over years, thought Devashish smiling to himself.

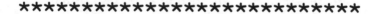

#16

'We will go to roam in the mall', suggested Shweta. It was 9.00 am in the morning and Anuranjini had dozed only for half an hour in the night. Sleeping was an attribute she had totally forgotten.

'What would you like to have for breakfast?' asked Anuranjini bustling around. She had watered the plants and had done the morning chores. Vishwas had gone back home early in the morning.

'Anything', she replied smiling broadly, 'I can digest even iron and rust.'

'Sorry, unfortunately I don't keep that flavor here', smiled back Anuranjini, putting down her paper, 'You get ready, eat something that I will make and then we will leave. Don't you want to go to the college today?'

'Nope', replied Shweta brightly, 'Today is mass bunk day!'

Anuranjini laughed shaking her head. Mass bunk was the most favorite thing of her college life. Whenever there was a mass bunk, she and Shiven would go to the library and go through millions of books.

The good old times, chuckled Anuranjini to herself.

'Shiven will you please listen to me this once?' begged Anuranjini.

'Yeah', said Shiven, perusing his planner, 'I am listening. Shoot whatever you want to say.'

'Look', said Anuranjini patiently, 'Rishabh is not that bad a guy. That day he said that sometimes I should spend time with some other classmates also apart from you. And frankly speaking; don't you think he has got a point? Since last three years we have been the best friends; the inseparable duo. It doesn't hurt if I spend a very little time with another fellow classmate, right? He is not asking me out for a movie or coffee; he just wants to learn some concepts of radioactivity from me. If you say no, I won't teach him. But these days he is down to begging and I hate when someone does like that.'

'Go', said Shiven without an expression, 'If I stop you; you will feel bad for him. You will roam around the college with a heavy heart; it's okay. You go and teach him radioactivity. We'll exchange notes in the evening. I will come to your place.'

'Shiven', said Anuranjini aghast, 'Why are you doing this to me? It is as if you are sentencing me to death. If you won't send me without your wish, I never will get over my conscious. Please Shiven.'

'Andy', said Shiven gazing at her intently, 'Don't seriously bother about me. I have some other jobs to accomplish for mom. You carry on with Ri . . . him and then we will meet in the evening. Now please leave without creating much melodrama or rather I am leaving.'

Shiven swung his bag over his shoulder and walked over to his vehicle at the parking opposite to the science department. Anuranjini just sat there; her mind completely blank. She was wondering what she would do next when a voice said,

'Hello gorgeous! I am here. But where is Mr. Fear?'

'His name is Shiven, Rishabh', said Anuranjini, 'Have you brought your books?'

'No', replied Rishabh swinging his keys stylishly, 'I am quite sure you have brought yours. Won't you share your books with me?'

Anuranjini stared at him and he winked back.

'Better still I will bring a coffee', he said, 'I haven't eaten a morsel since morning.'

Before Anuranjini could utter a word, Rishabh had left in the blink of an eye. Anuranjini opened her book, her notes and readied everything so that when he returned she could start teaching him. And indeed, when he returned he seemed to have returned with what seemed like half the cafeteria. Anuranjini looked aghast as she saw only one hand, a bit of his fringe and two feet walking *towards her. The rest of the Rishabh was hidden behind the entire collection of food. He came over to her and toppled the food that was duly wrapped, beside her and grimaced as he stretched himself. They were seated in the garden overlooking the Sayajigunj Road—in the distance the meager traffic could be seen flashing away.*

'I didn't know that when you miss a meal you get so wild for food', said Anuranjini still not able to get over her shock.

'Oh no', he smiled mischievously; 'We both can share. If you can share your books then I definitely can share food Anuranjini. Food comes with a price, knowledge is priceless.'

Anuranjini stared at him disbelievingly. He was a fellow who never really bothered about studies or books. Every year some or other of his girlfriends had been instrumental behind his clearing the final exams. He was such an over-confident fellow that even studies never seemed to bother him. But seeing him praise books and knowledge and science was just so more than enough that Anuranjini was having difficulty in making sure if she was sitting with the same careless Rishabh.

Nevertheless teach him Radioactivity—thought Anuranjini.

By the end of the session, Rishabh had started dozing off. Anuranjini kept prodding him but still he could hardly keep his eyes open. When she finally got tired, she collected her books and notes, highly offended, stuffed them haphazardly into her bag and left from there, muttering to herself;

Shiven is always right. This idiot will never realize the beauty of this subject.

When Rishabh opened his eyes, he saw an angry Anuranjini leaving at a top speed. The wafers, chips, finger-chips; all were untouched and Anuranjini's speed was alarming. Rishabh ran behind her.

'What happened Anuranjini?' gasped Rishabh catching up with her.

'You are really a big fool!' yelled Anuranjini, 'No. Sorry, I am the biggest fool. How could I even think that you will want to learn Physics and something as tough as Radioactivity? You don't have respect for anything. I have better jobs to do and yet I spare some time for you and you shamelessly doze while I am trying to make you understand the subject! Shiven was right; people like you will never understand anything and be serious.'

'Anuranjini come on!' said Rishabh exasperatedly, 'Give me a break. Why do you think I wanted to study Radioactivity? I don't want to learn it. I just wanted to spend some time with you. The study session was just an excuse; the reality is that I wanted to be close to you because I love you Anuranjini.'

There was a momentary long silence after the greatest proclamation of the millennium.

'Oh wow!' said Anuranjini sarcastically, 'How many girls have you told this to? Do you think that I am blissfully unaware of it all? I may be a studious geek but not that absolute fool. Just go away Rishabh; just leave me and my life in peace!'

'I won't', said Rishabh standing in front of her, 'I want to know what you think of me.'

'I think that you are a major show off!' said Anuranjini angrily, 'Take my answer; I hate you!'

Anuranjini left at a fantastic speed, her hair swaying behind her as the sun shone it black. Rishabh stood there, angry. No girl had ever denied him or his company and here is Anuranjini who had bluntly said no to him on his face. God, I love her; said Rishabh to himself.

I hate him God, said Anuranjini holding the handle of her vehicle and breathing deeply.

'What happened didi?' said Shweta, a bit scared, 'You burned the breakfast. Anything wrong; why are you breathing so heavily? I will take care of the food. You take rest didi.'

Anuranjini realized she was sweating and breathing with difficulty and the food was burning in front of her in the pan. She went to the bathroom to wash her face and her breathing turned back to normal.

God, I hate him; thought Anuranjini angrily.

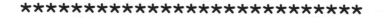

✱✱✱✱✱✱✱✱✱✱✱✱✱✱✱✱✱✱✱✱✱✱✱✱

#17

The guest lecture ended and many students crowded around Devashish to ask him doubts and question him on most impossible things to happen in the world. Devashish was very patient and was really interested to answer some of the mind boggling questions. *The student crop over the years have improved;* smiled Devashish to himself. When finally he was through with them all, he left the classroom with an extra spring in his step. He realized at the end of the session that his knowledge over some facts too, had increased. That is why he always liked such interactive sessions and if the students were such an interested lot, the sessions were always fun.

He went to the H.O.D's cabin once more before leaving, sat discussing for ten minutes and then left. Not deciding what to do, he thought he would take a long walk of the area. He wanted to be acquainted with the city where he would be living for the next few weeks.

It is not like how it used to be when we had come here few years back; thought Devashish.

Devashish and his parents lived in Sangamner, a small town in Maharashtra and only few years back had they shifted to Vadodara after his dad's transferable job. Within a short time he had left for Dehradun and then consequently for Frankfurt. He felt he never knew Vadodara at all.

He caught an auto and got into it.

'Where to sahib?' asked the driver.

'Wherever you say', said Devashish, heavily, 'I want a ride.'

'Then we have a very short distance', said the driver, 'The Alkapuri area and the Inox and stuff. You may like it. You get all weird and strange types there.'

'Well, then we can head off', said Devashish.

Devashish liked the ride. The auto driver was right. There were crazy and strange types of people. Devashish suddenly knew why; mostly the entire populace was of youngsters, some off the college, some bunking, some with families and pretty silent too. He got down the auto and decided to go over to the Café Coffee Day there. The auto driver gave the entire details of the place. Devashish paid the fare and thanking him, left.

He grabbed the handle of the door and pushed open the glass door. He stood there at the doorway for a long minute. A waiter came over to him,

'Good afternoon sir. How can I help you?'

'Good afternoon', said Devashish replying back, 'I was just thinking . . .'

'. . . sir!' squealed a voice excitedly. Devashish saw the person in concern.

Anish came waltzing towards him. He was in such a momentum that Devashish thought he might not directly land on top of him. Anish managed to skid to a halt in front of him.

'Please do join us', he insisted smiling very broadly so much that Devashish was scared that his grinders might not enter his eyes and turning to the waiter, 'He is a great teacher and a researcher. Just came from Frankfurt few days back.'

The waiter touched his cap respectfully.

'Yes Anish', said Devashish quite sure the whole Café was seeing the episode interestedly, 'Please don't make a national announcement of it. I will join you.'

The three settled down; Devashish Shastri, Anish and Vedika. Anish was bubbling with so much excitement that he was hardly able to sit in his chair.

'Anish', said Devashish weakly, 'Why don't you settle down properly? I am getting tired seeing you jump like that.'

'Yes sir', said Anish and still getting more energetic, 'It is not everyday a student gets to sit down and talk with a teacher, let alone a visiting faculty. I am hardly able to contain my happiness.'

Vedika too seemed to share the same excitement and both stared at the scholar as if he was a new blend of coffee of the Café.

'How come you reached here immediately after the lecture?' asked Devashish.

'Just like that', he replied, 'I told you I enjoy and study, both. I felt like coming here so I and Vedika came over. I never in the whole world thought that I may come across you over here.'

Devashish smiled back at the young fellow. He had been very comfortable with the boy ever since he had met up with him at the tarmac at the airport. He never knew that he would see more of him ever. *Something is cooking god, please tell me;* said Devashish to himself.

#18

It was Friday and Anuranjini was packing up as she had to leave for Vadodara by evening. That day, apart from Vishwas and Shweta, Anuranjini had Nimesh's and Vani's company too. Everyone was assisting and cleaning up—the flat was going to remain locked for a few weeks.

'My coffee still remains on hold', said Nimesh morosely.

Anuranjini laughed loudly, 'We'll have a coffee. How about this noon? Before my train?'

'Yeah that will be best', said Vani brightly, 'He won't eat both of ours head. Just go with him once Anuranjini. He is a real bugger otherwise.'

'Otherwise', said Shweta, 'Why don't you three go together? I need to clear up this place. I will be peaceful for some time. I have so much work. Vishwas has to go to meet his boss. Will you all please leave me in peace and not disturb me? I want a bit of thorough cleaning and possibly an anti-bacterial drive to establish.'

'Shut up Shweta', said Vishwas, through gritted teeth.

'Shweta has a point', said Nimesh thoughtfully, 'Come on girls ready up. We will leave for a coffee. Vish you get along with your work. We will return here at around two. Anuranjini has got to catch her train too. Come on, come on. No work delay.'

And that is what they did. The three left for the Nimesh's much wailed coffee and Vishwas had half an hour's job to finish at his boss's place. Shweta turned the song on full, started cleaning up and jumping around; a thing that she loved to do. Vishwas turned to look at Anuranjini's place and said,

'I am scared. You have given the entire charge in the hands of a tornado expecting it to stay calm', said Vishwas as the beats of the music reverberated in the lobby.

'Vishwas', said Anuranjini smiling broadly, 'Shweta is like my own sister. Even if she does some capital damage, there is nothing there that I will lose. Trust me; I am very happy you introduced me to her.'

Vishwas smiled back. Talking to Anuranjini felt nice. She was so subtle. *What in the world made Rishabh take this decision?* thought Vishwas.

The coffee was a real hilarious session as the coffee somehow didn't go through Nimesh's throat but all its way down to his pants. Vani burst out into laughter and Anuranjini had to order another one and ask someone to clear up the whole mess. Nimesh was totally ashamed of himself. It had happened accidentally. He was describing a scene to Vani that had happened in office and he was describing it so animatedly that his hand banged against his cup and the entire coffee was on him. He went to the bathroom to clean up.

'He always is like that', said Vani laughing and shaking her head, 'That was why I insisted you two to go. I got dragged into this scene.'

Anuranjini smiled, 'A very genuine person I daresay. He is fun if you have him around.'

'That's true', said Vani smiling back, 'I am glad I have a very loving fellow. He is very responsible person and the perfect someone with whom you would like to spend time or spend your whole life.'

'He is', said Anuranjini, giggling, 'When in office everyone knew that I was going to get divorced, the whole office used to stare at me as if it was entirely my fault. My condition was getting deteriorated and only Nimesh knew that there was something wrong. Nimesh was the only one who never changed his behavior with me and perhaps the only person who knows the truth. I am really glad that he didn't change. I am happy I have such a great colleague working with me.'

Nimesh came back and was comparatively silent and Vani and Anuranjini had a good laugh as he morosely stared at them, sipping his coffee.

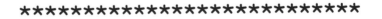

✶✶✶✶✶✶✶✶✶✶✶✶✶✶✶✶✶✶✶✶✶✶✶✶✶

Around 1.30 pm, the entire gang left to drop Anuranjini to the station. Everyone was silent except for Shweta who was chatting with Anuranjini. Anuranjini found it funny; some of the incidents Shweta had to relate. Vishwas was just staring at his own sister; *Anuranjini is right,*

Shweta is a marvelous person. I don't even know my sister I think. Vani and Nimesh were just exchanging few words as Nimesh drove.

Anuranjini didn't have much to carry; just two small bags. The train's arrival was announced and in a distance there was a hoot. Anuranjini turned to them all and hugged everyone in turn before she could board. When she hugged Vishwas she burst into tears. Vishwas held her closely and soothed her,

'You get rid of that wastrel', said Vishwas softly, 'Be strong and fight him off. Give us all the good news. He is not that worth that you waste your precious tears for him. Just be you.'

'Thank you Vishwas', wept Anuranjini into his shoulder, 'You have supported a lot in the last few days. You hardly knew me and still you did a lot for me. I don't think I ever will be able to repay you. Thanks for everything.'

'Hey girl', said Vishwas, 'Go now. Your train does not understand our position at the moment. When all the proceedings end do give a call and tell us that you are free of that monster for a lifetime. Take care.'

Anuranjini boarded the train and waved to all of them, through a tear-stained face. The train gained momentum and was soon out of sight. Anuranjini pushed her way through the crowd and stood towards the inside of the compartment. One of the seated elderly men saw her condition and made some space for her to sit down. She thanked him and sat down.

'The next stop will be at Anand', he said, mildly, 'I will get down there. You sit comfortably, okay?

You don't seem to be in a good condition. Are you unwell?'

'Yes', she replied smiling, 'A bit of cough and fever.'

'You be careful young one', he said, 'Sit down comfortably after I leave.'

Anuranjini smiled back. *All kindness in the world cannot be gone;* thought Anuranjini. The Anand station slid into view in some time and the man left. Anuranjini sat comfortably. She saw huge bunches of kids boarding the train; mostly commuters and some returning home early. They all were in one huge gang; giggling, chatting, listening to music, pulling each other's legs and making total chaos. Anuranjini smiled to herself, *youngsters.*

#19

Rishabh was wondering what to do. He wanted to pack up so that by the next day's early morning train, he could leave for Vadodara. *Today is Friday night;* thought Rishabh; *I will hang out somewhere.* He quickly put few pairs of clothes and his few necessary accessories in his bag and closed it with a flourish. Generally he used to hang out with Vishwas—both used to either go to the old city side for some tasty food or watch a movie and go gaming. Within a week, lot had changed and he knew his life was going to change the next week. Suddenly his phone rang and he picked it up. It was from his,

'Mom!' he exclaimed, 'I am coming home tomorrow.'

'Really?' said Mrs. Joshi curtly, 'I didn't ask you when you are coming home.'

'What are you saying mom? Aren't you happy that I am coming home?' said Rishabh aghast.

'Why not beta?' replied Mrs. Joshi sarcastically, 'You will come and my daughter-in-law will leave us all forever. I will never forgive you ever for what have you done to her. You have destroyed her completely. It was you who had in the first place come to me saying you wanted to marry her and then you are the one who is throwing her out of your own life.'

'Mom . . .'

'If you are coming then you can come home', said Mrs. Joshi, sobbing, 'You are my son Rishabh and that is one fact even I cannot erase. I will never be able to face Anuranjini or her parents for the wrong you did to her.'

Saying she cut the line. Rishabh was taken aback. He was not ready to believe that even his mother didn't support him. He got upset and decided not to go anywhere. He knew he wasn't going to get any support from home—but he knew he didn't love Anuranjini anymore. The initial thrill, the excitement on seeing her, the happiness and joy—he didn't feel anything of it at all. Sitting idly at his home, he switched on his TV. As he saw the images cross the screen, his eyes drooped and he fell asleep.

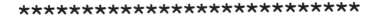

★★★★★★★★★★★★★★★★★★★★★★★★

#20

From that day all hell broke loose in Anuranjini's life. Wherever she went, Rishabh was always there. Smiling mischievously, staring, and gazing at her intently. Anuranjini got more and more conscious. She never breathed a word about these incidents or her effort to teach radioactivity to Shiven else she was sure there would be a war.

'What is this Rishabh up to these days?' quizzed Shiven one day as they sat solving sums in the library, 'Did you teach Radioactivity with so much interest that he has decided to mend his ways?'

'You can say so if you wish', muttered Anuranjini. She was highly disturbed these days by Rishabh's never ending chase around the campus. Ever since she and Shiven had decided that they won't discuss Rishabh, it had been a numbed pain in the corner of her mind. She was glad of not having to discuss him with Shiven, yet so much was bottled inside her that she didn't know whom she should turn to remove the poison from her system.

Not that Shiven wasn't noticing all that was going on, but he was under the impression *that Rishabh had finally decided to improve his lackadaisical way and get serious with life.*

Maybe he really wants to score this time; thought Shiven.

'Is everything alright?' asked Shiven staring at her, 'You seem to be disoriented Anuranjini. Something is not okay.'

'No I am fine', said Anuranjini, shaking her head, 'I want something.'

'What thing?' said Shiven; he was getting scared looking at Anuranjini. She never really told anybody anything and he was dead sure she was suppressing something.

'I want to eat something', she replied. Food was always a great cover up these days, 'I will get a sandwich. I am dead hungry. I can hardly pay attention to what I am doing.'

'Shall I get you one?' said Shiven still scared. Anuranjini was less of replying to him and more of muttering to herself.

'No, I will get one', said Anuranjini, 'I can take a walk around too. It may make me feel better.'

Shiven nodded and Anuranjini exited. Shiven watched her leave and instantly saw Rishabh leaving from the table opposite to them. Shiven rounded off his calculations as he adjusted his specs.

Anuranjini ran on in full throttle. She decided to get a cup of tea and eat something at the outlet outside the library. She knew Rishabh was following her and she wanted to escape him too. The real reason for her uneasiness was the hangover she was having and a constant fear of Rishabh chasing her. Rishabh's methods were really beginning to scare her more than irking her.

'One coffee and a sandwich please', she said at the counter.

'Make it two', said a voice behind her.

'Rishabh please . . .' turned Anuranjini with an obvious irritation and then froze in her tracks, 'Shiven, you?'

'Not pleased to see me, are you?' said Shiven with a cut of an ice in his tone, 'Rishabh is waiting for you at the entrance of the library.'

Anuranjini seemed terminally horrified to see Shiven standing there in front of her. The expression on her face was of utter surprise and shock. She froze with big and round eyes. Her breathing choked and she temporarily stilled her supply. Shiven patted on her cheek mildly to make sure she just hadn't managed to freeze herself to death.

'Shiven . . . I . . .' muttered Anuranjini but stopped short.

'Andy, why didn't you tell me that Rishabh was not really learning seriously but chasing you since so long?' said Shiven. His voice was peaceful but it was this peace that was breaking her into pieces.

'Two coffees', announced the waiter.

'Shiven', she gasped for air, 'I didn't want you to go and pick a fight with him. Promise me you won't do that. I won't forget the last time—I don't want another fight. I am really scared.'

'Andy', said Shiven taking the coffees, 'Trust me. I won't go picking a fight with Rishabh anymore. I realized something; between you and me we will never discuss Rishabh. What with only ten days left for our final exams, we don't have time and space for rubbish discussion, agreed?'

Anuranjini nodded her head and heaved a sigh of relief. It was nice to see Shiven talking about non-violence. Her biggest fear had always been that if Shiven came to know that since months, Rishabh had been chasing her; there would be the biggest war of all times and bloodshed. She didn't want that happening. Rishabh was very adamant and was not ready to give up on Anuranjini. He hadn't thrown a glance at any other girl in so many months. He was all bent on breaking down Anuranjini's wall of patience. So far Anuranjini had been patient and strong. She knew internally she would break sooner or later. Her strength was giving away and one of these days if Rishabh asked her, she might even say yes.

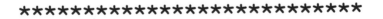

The exams began at The Maharaja Sayajirao University and the atmosphere too seemed to feel sorry for the kids but then rejoiced at the idea of the exams ending soon and that there will be worry free youngsters. The leaves rustled mildly in the wind and the sun was throwing flashlights in between the branches. There was silence and there was noise at the same time; there was ambush and there was peace together. The atmosphere got confused as to what it should do; should it commemorate or should it be mild?

There is always something of exams that is always tied up with time. When the exams didn't begin, each day dragged itself and there were times when students literally tried to kill time. But when the exams began, someone had to do something to stop it before the week ended. The exam weeks flew faster than any mountain wind.

'I don't feel like I have appeared for any exam', squealed Anuranjini, jumping and punching the air, 'It seems like only yesterday I had come for the first paper and look, today was the last paper. It is over! We are free.'

'Yes', smiled Shiven. He was really very tired and he had hardly eaten or slept during the exams, 'Finally. I am planning to go to Jaipur for one week. I am dead tired. I have not eaten a morsel since weeks it seems.'

'Why Jaipur?' asked Anuranjini, puzzled. When had the Jaipur plan been made!

'Just like that', he said wiping his forehead, 'I am planning for a week with mom and dad or I may go alone also. My uncle lives there. It will be worth a visit after the exams.'

'Sounds good', said Anuranjini. Her hair was flying behind her, her eyes had circles and she seemed very weak. But something she couldn't contain was her happiness that the toughest type of exams ever she had faced was finally over, 'Do send me a post card and take lots of pictures and for gods' sake don't take your pictures; take pictures of the surroundings.'

The two walked over to the parking to get to their vehicles. Shiven had some work to do and Anuranjini decided to leave for home. Shiven left in a hurry and Anuranjini stood talking to some of her friends from statistics and mathematics department. Parita came running towards her, all breathless.

'Here you are', she said holding her for oxygen, 'Everyone is in the classroom. There's a small Physics department get-together.'

'Wait then I will call Shiven', said Anuranjini extracting her mobile from her bag.

'No', said Parita suddenly alarmed, 'Don't call him.'

Anuranjini stared at her with a mild frown.

'Alright', said Parita, 'Rishabh is calling you there alone. He says he wants to talk about something to you and won't rest until he doesn't. He said that he really wants to meet you.'

Anuranjini lost her temper, 'Parita, are you mine or his friend? I am not going to Rishabh and go and tell that "new friend" of yours that I won't meet him and definitely not alone. If he needs to talk to me then he will have to do so in front of Shiven. I have had enough!'

Parita stared at her, 'What the hell on round earth is the problem?'

'Rishabh has been proposing to me every single day since last eight months', said Anuranjini, 'I am fed up of the fellow . . .'

'. . . wait a minute', said Parita, 'Since last eight months? Do you know what that means? He may be having some idea more than ordinary past time love.'

'Marriage?' quizzed Anuranjini, her eyes narrowing.

Parita nodded, 'He has never chased any girl this long. He hasn't given upon you which means that there is more to this love, if it happens. Just go and talk to him Anuranjini and get things cleared. End this suffocation and get yourself some air. Trust me, you will feel better after that.'

'You mean I should go', said Anuranjini.

'Yes', replied Parita nodding her head matter-of-factly.

Anuranjini decided that she would go to meet Rishabh ultimately and end it all. Parita had been right—the only sensible thing was to end the suffocation and get some air. She walked towards their classroom and she saw Rishabh seated on the first bench with his head down.

Anuranjini stepped on the threshold and listening to her foot fall, he raised his head.

'Hi', he smiled tiredly.

'Hi', she replied without emotion.

'I just want to talk to you about something', he said, 'That is why I asked Parita to tell you a lie.'

'She didn't tell me any lies', said Anuranjini, shaking her head, 'I decided to come here and finish it all.'

'*I wish to start*', said Rishabh, '*This is not the end Anuranjini. I just want to tell you that I am really serious for you. You are right; I have said such things to many girls in my life. But you are the first one in all these times for whom I have felt like that. I didn't look at any other girl in all these months and for the first time I sat and studied. I know my impression isn't that good but I never did anything wrong to any girl Anuranjini. Even it was Kavya who broke off with me. I am just not simply serious—I mean every word I am saying. I want to marry you Anuranjini. I have also told my mom and dad about you and shown some of the college function photos. They have already accepted you as their daughter-in-law. They are waiting for your answer so that they can come to your home and ask your parents for your hand in marriage. They don't want to force you into this marriage Anuranjini. But I know one thing for sure, if I don't marry you, I never will be able to marry another woman ever in my life.*'

Anuranjini stood there transfixed by the end of it. She had never in the entire universe thought that Rishabh was serious enough to marry her. She felt that he just wanted an on and off affair and then as usual have a break-up and carry on further in life.

'*Rishabh*', she started slowly, '*I don't know what to do or say. I am just so speechless.*'

'*Are you in love with Shiven?*' asked Rishabh.

'*No.*'

'*I thought so*', said Rishabh, '*Because I have never seen you both having anything romantic to talk except for Physics. He never says anything except for that. You both are, no doubt, the best friends. There isn't an aura of friendship between you two; it more or less is like a contract of Physics that you both are sharing just because you both have signed it.'*

'Rishabh', said Anuranjini icily, 'Keep Shiven out of this. Don't you dare to comment on our friendship! We share something more than Physics and that you won't understand.'

'I am sorry Anuranjini', said Rishabh a bit taken aback at her snappish reply.

Anuranjini continued staring at Rishabh as if in a trance and she was not uttering a word at all.

'I don't know about Shiven either', said Rishabh, now very silent and polite, 'But I do know that I love you very much and I wish to spend my life with you.'

Anuranjini had become stone silent and Rishabh came forward. She wasn't making even a single movement; she wasn't even blinking her eyes. He came, grabbed her shoulders and shook her mildly; she didn't move. He again shook her,

'Do wake up madam', said a young boy, 'The Vadodara station has arrived. All passengers have left. This train doesn't go any further.'

Anuranjini shook her head and woke out of her nap and saw that the compartment was slowly emptying around them. The young boy along with his gang had seen Anuranjini in deep nap and felt that she might not wake up soon enough to get down from the train. So he had waited back and shook her awake.

'We reached Vadodara?' asked Anuranjini not ready to believe her eyes. A slice of sunlight fell on her face and she shaded her eyes.

'Yes madam', he replied, 'This train will go back to Ahmadabad and leaves around 6.15 pm. I hope you don't want to go back.'

'Thank you', said Anuranjini smiling at the young boy. She grabbed her bags and disembarked from the train. It was evening and the evening rush at the Vadodara station was overwhelming. The intercity connecting further towards Surat was at the opposite platform. Many people were crowding, pushing, laughing and some even shouting abuses as they tried to grab a place inside the train.

Nothing is permanent in life; said Anuranjini to herself; *even I used to be happy once. I traded my life and happiness for nothing. I made a raw deal.*

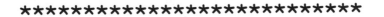

#21

It was Sunday and Devashish was getting ready. He had to go to see a girl named Meera. His elder brother, his sister, parents were all excited and they were creating more than necessary noise. He got irritated by the end of it,

'Mom Sit down!' he ordered, 'Malvika Shut up! Dad settle now!'

They all giggled and became silent. He heaved deeply and had a glass of water.

'Why are you all making so much noise and mess?' he said, 'Can't you act your age?'

When finally all was silent and set, they left for Meera's home. The meeting was supposed to be next week but Meera's company was sending her to Bangalore for training. The developments were so sudden that they decided to pre-pone the meeting.

Devashish got into the car and settled next to his brother at the front. He was feeling very weird. He felt he was going to see some altogether a different species, the one that is never found on earth. He didn't even know what to talk to her and how he should start. He thought that mostly he would pass out if the meeting turned out to be quite a huge event. He was, frankly, not in a mental state to go to see any girl. He knew however that if he came to India, this would be an unavoidable circumstance. India is indeed famous for two of the very important things; culture and agriculture. He didn't know much about the latter but about the former he was well aware. He knew marriage was an indispensable phase. He wished he was in Frankfurt. He felt he was better off there. Angie was the only woman he had ever seen apart from his mom, sister and sister-in-law.

He chuckled to himself; *I cannot marry a middle aged woman who is already married.*

'Are you happy or not?' asked Dhyanesh as he drove.

'I don't know', replied Devashish, 'I feel as if I am not mentally ready. I don't have a sensation of anything around me. It is as if I was never meant to marry and get into the conventional stuff.'

'That is strange', said Dhyanesh as he took a turn, 'Why cannot you marry? What is going on in your mind Devu?'

'Frankly speaking', said Devashish, 'Nothing. Nothing whatsoever is going on in my mind. I am all blank by gods' sake.'

'That is a good sign', said Dhyanesh, 'Just be normal and all will be well. We have for our own safety told them that you are like a nutty studious teacher. She is mentally prepared to face you. So should you be.'

I think I became mental only once in my life; thought Devashish smiling to himself.

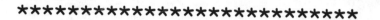

#22

Anuranjini turned to go home and knew for the first time that she had no notes to prepare, nothing to study or anything else to do that would keep her mind away from what Rishabh had told her. She was suddenly feeling heavy headed and then she realized why; for the first time she wanted to believe that Rishabh had spoken a true word about love and life. He was serious about her and wanted to carry on with her as a life partner.

Can this be true? Wondered Anuranjini; Does he really want to marry me or is it all a gimmick just so that he gets even with me for what Shiven did to him? Am I being stupid because this is Rishabh! How can I possibly assume that he is speaking the truth? But then he must be really serious—who knows. If I agree, what will Shiven think? Will he boycott? Shiven! I should go to him.

She sped her way to Shiven's home but he hadn't reached yet. He still was out with his mother's errands. She decided to wait for him. She waited a painful half an hour after which Shiven finally landed there. He came in whistling and punching the air celebrating that the exams had finally ended. When he had left the campus he was wondering wistfully how the three years had passed with Physics and Anuranjini. Both were preparing now for Masters and were dreaming for Faculty of Technology that held the masters courses too. Though they would be together, nothing could change the essence of youth that Bachelors degree brought with it—Masters was a serious deal.

When he had entered, he had hardly paid attention that Anuranjini was sitting there. He kept all the packets on the dining table and was chatting nonchalantly with his mother when she pointed out a sitting Anuranjini. Shiven jumped a little.

'Hello little girlie', he addressed, 'When did you come?'

'Actually half an hour ago', said Anuranjini. She seemed close to tears. One look at her and Shiven came to know the entire trouble. It had, no doubt, something to do with Rishabh. His "judgmental nose", as he called it, sniffed Rishabh out from the aura around her.

'I don't want to listen to what you have got to say', said Shiven, 'We are going to Rishabh's place right now!'

Anuranjini gave an astonished expression: Best Friend indeed. He always smells out the problem!

Both left at top speed. Shiven drove while Anuranjini patiently sat behind him. She seemed to have got temporarily frozen in the heat of the summer. Shiven was very cool; he knew he had to keep a rare attribute in his pocket, patience. He knew what the problem was already; Rishabh had proposed to her and she was not sure if she really loved him. When they reached Rishabh's home, Shiven called out to him.

'Shiven here', said Shiven. 'I need to talk to you.'

Rishabh stood at the balcony completely transfixed.

'Please come up', requested Rishabh.

'No, I won't', said Shiven firmly, 'Sorry dude, but I won't step in there.'

Rishabh sighed and came down, opened the gate and stood there waiting for Shiven's firing.

'You proposed to Anuranjini, right?' asked Shiven, still firmly.

'Didn't she tell you?' said Rishabh surprised.

'She hasn't spoken a word since last one hour I guess', said Shiven, 'I am merely assuming that is what has happened.'

'You are the truest friend to Anuranjini', said Rishabh smiling, 'Yes. I proposed to Anuranjini not only for love, but also for marriage. Shiven, I have decided. I am ending this entire gimmick games; endless flirting and all. I have finally decided to settle down. I am in love with Anuranjini and I have showed her photos to mom and dad and they loved her and are waiting when they have to go to her place to ask her hand in marriage.'

Rishabh paused and took a breather.

'I hope you are not revenging me Rishabh for what Shiven did to you', said Anuranjini scared.

'No', said Rishabh, feeling his cheeks, 'I think I really was irritating then. I should not meddle with anyone who is trying to solve out numerical *sums in Physics. That is something I realized after I solved some myself. I am sorry buddy.'*

Shiven put a hand on Rishabh's shoulder, 'I too am sorry dude. I have no other complain. If you are intending to marry Anuranjini in the decent way, I have nothing more to ask or say. Enjoy holidays.'

Anuranjini stared at Shiven as he swerved his vehicle and turned. Within a short time they were out of Rishabh's sight. Anuranjini caught herself thinking about Rishabh; the guy who really wanted to marry her and hadn't looked at another girl in the last eight months and for her, he had seriously studied for the exams. He had even attended the quiz competition which she and Shiven had won. I haven't given Shiven the photo we had taken with the judge and the head of department; chuckled Anuranjini to herself. She decided to take a decision and tell Shiven.

'Shiven stop the vehicle', said Anuranjini patting him on his shoulder lightly.

Shiven stopped his bike.

'I have decided something', said Anuranjini as Shiven half turned his head back, 'I am telling mom and dad. I have decided to marry Rishabh. He is all that childish and silly right now. I think I know; I also have developed a liking for him.'

Shiven turned to face Anuranjini and the expression was that of shock, disgust and disbelief. He didn't utter another word and drove to his place. As soon as both disembarked, Anuranjini got to her vehicle and turned to Shiven.

'I am not making a mistake Shiven', she said, *'I want you to be a part of this entire event. Won't you be?'*

Shiven shook his head, *'No Anuranjini. Bye.'*

Anuranjini was shocked as Shiven went inside and slammed the door shut. She started her vehicle and left; not ready to believe that Shiven had out rightly said no on her face. Not only had he not behaved strangely, he had not spoken more than two or three lines which was really strange. She wanted him to scream and shout and let his anger out but he had gulped everything and had not even let out fumes. More than his words, his silence was killing her and she was not ready to take that—not from Shiven.

'Andy come on', said Shantanu, prodding his sister, 'Will you finally eat your breakfast? It is getting cold.'

Anuranjini stared at the food on the plate kept in front of her. The pedestal fan was revolving frequently throwing wind on her face.

I made the biggest mistake; thought Anuranjini; *May be that is why Shiven didn't say a word to me then. He was heart-broken to see me acting the usual fool. He had explained to me a lot. Anyway, I am rectifying the error tomorrow. There is always an error of plus or minus five accepted in Physics. This has been six years; no idea if it is acceptable or not.*

#23

Monday appeared very beautiful. There was huge sun and a cool wind blowing. The leaves rustled and some leaves rolled on the roads until they got crushed. All vehicles were flying left and right. The conditions were all perfect for the perfect day; even perfect for a perfect ending.

Rishabh and his family and Anuranjini's family appeared ten minutes before the due time at the domestic court to sign the papers and break off the marriage. Rishabh's parents were feeling ashamed and weren't even facing Anuranjini. Rishabh was the only one who was jubilant enough. When all the legalities ended on a peaceful note, the judge asked Anuranjini,

'Do you wish to claim anything from Mr. Rishabh Joshi?'

Anuranjini smiled and shook her head, 'No sir. Thank you. I don't want to claim anything at all. Everything is settled.'

The judge nodded.

The families and the two left the courtroom and walked into the sunlight. Anuranjini squinted as the sunlight resplendently drenched her and Rishabh shaded his eyes and turned to talk to his parents.

Anuranjini smiled and walked up to where Rishabh was standing, removing her wedding locket and holding it out to him said very slowly, 'My blessings to you and Madhvi for your next marriage. May nothing ever come between you both; not even you.'

Rishabh gave a very malicious stare while his parents scanned their toes. It was a very awkward moment but nothing could be done. Given it their way, they would never have let Anuranjini go. But Rishabh's behavior had turned a complete circle and Anuranjini's miseries had only worsened. They decided to call it quits considering Anuranjini's deteriorating health and never ending stress.

Anuranjini went to Rishabh's parents.

'I don't think I have a right to call you mom and dad anymore', she started, 'I just have one request to both of you. Please, do not scold or make Rishabh feel bad for this. This marriage was never meant to happen. It was a mistake we both made in the prime of our youth which we have corrected. After all we are students of Physics. We both are happy that this has happened and I have no regrets.'

Mrs. Joshi's eyes filled with tears. She patted her on her cheek, smiling.

'I will very soon meet you', said Anuranjini smiling again, 'If there ever comes a chance to meet you again.'

★★★★★★★★★★★★★★★★★★★★★★★★★

#24

Vishwas had hardly paid attention to anything in the past few days. Anuranjini had appeared before every vision; he had not seen anything else.

'If you mix the flour and eggs, really, mom will be displeased', remarked Shweta staring at the ceiling, clearly wishing to avoid looking Vishwas in the face.

'What?' he said disconcerted.

'Yeah', said Shweta pointing with her brows at the bowl in Vishwas's hand, 'This is not the right combination. We make chapattis with flour and we don't make eggetarian chapattis. Sorry.'

Vishwas threw a dirty look at Shweta as she gave a grimace back.

'You are in love with Anuranjini', said Shweta, giving a dirty smile. Cunningness was building a crooked smile on her otherwise beautiful countenance.

'What did you say?' said Vishwas picking up the frying pan and ready to launch at her.

'Don't do that', said Shweta with an uninterested look, 'I am not scared of all that. Your face says it all. Why don't you ask her and tell mom about Anuranjini? I liked her. She is just so normal even if she is so beautiful; not at all haughty. Heavens don't make such girls often; trust my words.'

Vishwas turned a bright shade of pink at Shweta's words. He smiled and gave her a friendly punch.

'I think for the first time I really want to listen to what my younger sister is saying', said Vishwas smiling.

Shweta winked back, 'You will make her a perfect groom. She could do with some humane treatment. That jerk; Rishabh; I hate him like anything. I am glad that girl is getting free of him once and for all.'

Immediately the phone rang. It was Anuranjini who had called to inform them about the proceedings. She seemed to be even more tired than usual and Vishwas didn't want to pressurize her to talk anymore. She quickly hung up and then Vishwas let out a whistle.

'I think I am all set', said Vishwas.

'Hey', said Shweta, amazed, 'You are blushing!'

'Boys don't blush Shweta', said Vishwas darkly.

'You are . . .'

Shweta could never complete that statement as Vishwas took the frying pan and finally launched after her. She was laughing around as the pair of them were running in circles and their mother had to intervene to pull them apart.

Anuranjini, be mine forever; wished Vishwas smiling to himself.

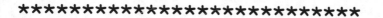

#25

On Tuesday morning, Anuranjini decided to take a round of the city. She didn't know why, but she felt like visiting the university where she had completed her graduation. *It is better I visit my past;* thought Anuranjini; *that is the place where it all started. I must visit it once so that I can put my ghosts to rest.*

Deciding that she would finally go to the University; she got ready and put on no make-up. She decided to wear a dress of white cotton. She liked cottons a lot. Supriya was to go to the office; so on the way she dropped Anuranjini at the University.

As soon as Anuranjini stepped in there, she had a weird feeling. A mild wind lifted her hair and ruffled her scarf. It was as if she had never left that place. One part of her had always been in the University. In the last six years, lots of changes had taken place. But there was something very nice about the feeling she felt within when she walked through the narrow paths. She wanted to visit the Science Departments but she was scared that she may not become weak from within.

Face it; she chided herself. With a last combined efforts of all energies within her, she decided to walk over to the Physics Department. She stepped on the threshold of the empty classroom and all memories of Rishabh proposing to her came forward in one wave. She was glad there wasn't any lecture going on there. She felt she would pass out. Had it been few years back, she would never have felt this weak. But after marriage to Rishabh, he had pulled out all good things from her like a parasite and she seemed to be just a living corpse except that she hadn't slept for many months properly. Mere dozes in between was something she was habituated to.

She stepped back and exited the classroom. She roamed around the department, those places where she and Shiven and the rest of the class used to enjoy life. Now some other students were enjoying it. *May they never take silly decisions in life god;* prayed Anuranjini.

She was just roaming around without any meaning when suddenly a particular gang of kids came out of some classroom. There was a lot of hustle and bustle and all were discussing excitedly. A younger man was the centre of the entire talk and he was talking and discussing with the students who were bubbling with excitement.

'Wow sir', exclaimed a boy, 'You are a genius!'

'No my boy', said the teacher, smiling, 'It is just quite normal. Now you guys hurry on I need to visit the Head before I leave.'

'See you tomorrow sir', cheered back the children.

The man waved and left in another direction; towards Anuranjini. She smiled at herself; *visiting faculties. It used to be fun attending such seminars.*

Suddenly, the young man tripped over a stone and his books and papers flew out of his hand. Anuranjini ran forward to help him out. They both didn't seem to have noticed each other. When they finally raised their heads to face each other, spoke Anuranjini,

'Here are your books, sir.'

'Thank you very much', he replied and then there was a universal moment of time warp.

The past and the present; the known and the unknown; the said and the unsaid; all mixed with each other and the two were travelling in the same vehicle of time and space and they seem to be getting lost in it more and more.

'Shiven?' spluttered out Anuranjini.

'Andy?' he whispered hoarsely.

One boy came running breathlessly, 'Devashish sir, the Head is not in the cabin. He had to leave for an urgent meeting.'

'Thank you Anish', said Devashish turning to the boy and smiling and then looking back at Anuranjini.

The boy smiled and ran away at the same top speed. They both turned to face each other. No words seem to come from either's mouth. It was as if they were conversing through silence. Both were shocked and were not ready to believe that they had met each other after such a long time. Shiven's eyes seemed to have frozen in his eye-socket while Anuranjini seemed to have momentarily stopped breathing.

'You are Devashish Shastri here', said Anuranjini slowly, 'How are you Shiven?'

'I am not Shiven anymore', said Devashish expressionless, 'Devashish is my actual name; Shiven is something that the whole world used to call me. Not any more—Shiven looked better as a college going student, not as a research guy. Please don't call me that—it seems very lame to call me Shiven.'

Anuranjini stood there still, unmoving. Finally, she opened her mouth, 'Shiven, why are you behaving like this? Am I not your best friend? I thought marriage or no marriage; friends remain friends Shiven. That is one fact which even you, yourself, had agreed once upon a time, hadn't you?'

'No point', said Devashish with a smile curling his lips, 'From now on I am Devashish Shastri and very soon if things work out in time, I might never be in this country at all. Please do allow me to clarify a lot of things; I won't prefer being called Shiven; we both cannot remain friends like school kids; we cannot be even acquaintances. This friendship was something that we abandoned some years back. Nothing is going to rekindle it.'

Anuranjini gaped at him. There was a huge bundle of questions she had to ask and she knew she would have to answer some questions. She could not believe that on meeting accidentally after so many years; Shiven had blown her off just like that. She could understand Shiven's bitterness but she couldn't bear it. She had never been able to bear it. How much ever bitter he was during college, it was only Anuranjini's meek, soft and smooth voice calling "Shiven" that soothed him and acted like an instant nerve depressant. Today things seemed to be stark opposite and seemed to be aggravating the situation.

'Can we sit and talk somewhere Devashish? I need to clarify a lot of things from my side too. This is the least I can do. I don't know if I have the right to ask or not; but can we meet today in the evening? We will part our ways and I promise you will never see more of me.'

Devashish aka Shiven paused a minute, heaved deeply and said, 'Okay. Today evening at 5.30 pm at Inox is where we'll meet.'

Anuranjini nodded and both left. Anuranjini didn't want to leave. She wanted to stand there and look at him—her friend from yesteryears. She was not ready to gulp and digest the moment. The same guy whose mornings used to begin by calling her up and saying "G'Mornin' Andy—Today's Physics specials . . ." or every time she beat him at a numerical-expression of pure mock venom; he seemed to have changed and adapted to a life without her. She once again saw Shiven walk away—*just like he had gone when he was through with explaining me about Rishabh.*

Anuranjini too walked away; a lot of things mixing up from past and present and future— Rishabh's love chase, Shiven's intellectual explanations, her marriage, Shiven's disappearance and her four years of most hazardous married life. *God, why has Shiven come back into my life?* Thought Anuranjini; *Why are you punishing me? Did I do that big a crime to him?*

#26

The three days of Anuranjini and Shiven's life had been the perilous ones of total mental torture. Shiven had the whole day—as they met since morning—tried to explain to her why she shouldn't marry Rishabh. He had been very patient and listened to Anuranjini's ranting. He didn't know what to say so that she stopped herself from falling into this pit. He knew life with any other person on earth was agreeable but definitely not Rishabh.

Finally, Shiven's patience gave away and he pulled his hair out. He had been the most patient guy for Anuranjini. Generally, for a person who lost temper at mere mock-provocation; this had been the acid test. He became so furious yet he had to control. He knew he had to else Anuranjini would burst into tears.

'That is it Andy', said Shiven frustrated, 'I am through with you not only in concern with this matter but also for this lifetime. Now no more advices; I am tired and have better jobs to do too.'

'What do you mean "this lifetime"?' said Anuranjini surprised.

'Andy, what do you think?' said Shiven scornfully, 'That after marriage I will walk into your house? It won't appear nice if a married woman keeps on socializing with her male best friend— we are living in reality and not movies where everything is fine. Come to think of it, your precious Rishabh will not appreciate it. Also, you are marrying Rishabh, Anuranjini; and on all accounts I hate him. Don't even think I will ever be in contact with you after this decision of yours. I am getting through with you forever. I hope after this marriage of yours we never meet in life. I can't bear the pain of it all. You are making a big mistake.'

'But Shiven, a person like Rishabh has not looked at another girl in almost a year. It's a huge feat . . .'

'Yes! And he is getting an award for that—you! You are marrying him, his biggest ego trophy. I don't wish to say that Andy, but I hope you don't realize it at a very bad price. He is twenty one like all of us and we can expect a level of maturity from him; so far I have not seen anything!'

There was a long pause.

'I am done, Andy, I am really done', said Shiven breathing heavily.

Anuranjini stared at him and nodded mutely. She never said a word against Shiven and whatever he said was like gods' testament for her—unchangeable and firm.

'One day', said Shiven getting up to leave, 'I will come to meet you. I have to give you two gifts—one for your engagement and the other for your marriage. That will be our last transaction ever.'

Shiven left saying this; his bag dangling over his shoulder. They had been seated at the University garden opposite to the library. Shiven had decided the place to meet. That was where they had met all three days.

It is okay Anuranjini; thought Shiven; I will learn to live without you. I thought we were not just friends; we were more than that. But I guess I was wrong. Just because Rishabh sang his way around you, you are all his. Its fine Anuranjini, I will manage. I will never tell you how much I love you. I guess I was slightly late in telling what I felt about you—that's okay! You be good and take care, young Andy.

He reached his vehicle and started it. Before leaving the parking; he turned and saw Anuranjini sitting alone and staring at him. She waved to him and he waved back; Bye Anuranjini, bye forever.

'Why doesn't this boy wake up?' shouted Mrs. Shastri from the kitchen.

Dhyanesh and Malvika feared they will have a sore throat trying to wake up Devashish. Finally, Malvika screamed,

'Wake up Shiven!'

Devashish's eyes snapped open and he glared furiously at Malvika.

'You never considered Devashish as your name at all Bhaiyya', said Malvika irritated, 'You still reciprocate to Shiven only even if you have prohibited us all from calling you that.'

Malvika threw a dirty look and left mumbling to herself.

It is a name I want to forget; said Devashish to himself; *Why has god brought this name back into my life? Why has god brought back my forgotten life at all?*

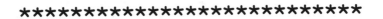

✶✶✶✶✶✶✶✶✶✶✶✶✶✶✶✶✶✶✶✶✶✶✶✶

#27

Anuranjini was so numb when she returned home that she didn't realize she was banging against a lot of things while walking. She somehow managed to walk her feet till the refrigerator and had water. Something in her told her she was a lot confused than earlier.

She wanted to say a lot of things and yet she wanted to hide a lot of things. She felt that a lot of mixing, confusing and unspeakable stuff was brewing and then it was falling back silent. It was as if the tides and ebbs in her heart were constantly stirring movement and her brain was not able to process it with the usual speed.

Her mother saw her condition and was intrigued. She knew something out of the blue had happened as this was the expression that she always carried ever since she was a kid when something unexpected popped up in her life.

'What is it Andy?' said Mrs. Roy, 'What has happened?'

'Mom', said Anuranjini slowly, 'It is all over with Rishabh and look the games fate plays with me. I met Shiven today after six long years. I don't know what to say mom, I am all confused and I have no idea how to react. Mom, why? Why has this happened?'

'All I can say', said Mrs. Roy sighing, 'Something between you and him is still left which needs to be finished. Until you don't end it, fate will keep on playing games with you.'

'I am ending it today in the evening', said Anuranjini breathing with difficulty, 'I have asked him to meet me and he agreed.'

Mrs. Roy glanced at her as if she was not sure about something.

****

#28

'Congratulations! I am really proud of you two', said the Head of the Department, 'You two are geniuses.'

'Thank you sir', said Anuranjini and Shiven bowing their head in humility.

'Let us go over for the photo session', said the head.

The three and other dignitaries assembled and the photographer who had been called took photos of the winners of the quiz competition. Though the two had won many competitions, this competition meant a lot for the two. This was their last competition in their college life. After this competition, the only next major event was the final exams.

'Thank you' said the photographer, 'The copies will be supplied at the head's cabin. You students can collect it from there.'

'I hope they give individual copies', said Shiven, 'I mean I hope I don't have to share my copy with you.'

'Don't you like sharing the photograph with me?' said Anuranjini, her eyes narrowing down.

'I don't like you', said Shiven slyly laughing, 'I only like the photograph. Please!'

'Laugh at me you idiot', said Anuranjini, 'When I will leave you and go; you will be the one who will miss me the most.'

Anuranjini laughed and ran and Shiven followed trying to hit her. They were running round in round in circles, Anuranjini laughing her head off. You are right; said Shiven; I will be the one who will miss you the most.

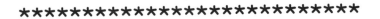

After a week, the photographs came and Anuranjini collected both the copies as Shiven was not feeling well and had taken the day off to go to the doctor.

In the evening when she came to Shiven's place, she kept on teasing him about the photograph.

'I won't give you your copy', she teased waving her thumb, 'Laughed at me, didn't you? Now I will never give you. Keep on begging.'

Shiven looked at her morosely as he lay in bed, coughing and wiping his nose.

Anuranjini kept laughing at him.

'Stop laughing at me', said Devashish angrily.

'I am not laughing', said a voice.

Someone shook him and he came out of his reverie. His brother Dhyanesh was standing over him. He was seated at the sofa and talking in sleep. Dhyanesh was in his room but on hearing his voice had come to investigate and found his younger brother mumbling in his sleep.

'Wake up Shiven', said Dhyanesh and left.

Don't call me Shiven; thought Devashish angrily; *I am Devashish Shastri. I hate the name Shiven. Why was my pet name Shiven?*

****

#29

The Inox multiplex is a regular hangout for all evening "let-outs". Everyone who wants to take a heavenly break from their work, problems as well as lives come over here to have a nice time. The moment you get into the basement there is an open air eatery and on the top floor you get all the screens showing the current box office hits or otherwise.

Youngsters found it fantastic and a convenient place to escape parental vigilance and have a memorable time with friends. Many families too came to Inox for a family outing and get-togethers.

Anuranjini knew she would never be able to sit there at home. So as early as possible she got ready and left for Inox. When she entered there, she saw Devashish standing at the top of the stairs to the basement. He hinted to her and she followed him downstairs.

They took a seat at the extreme end after ordering two coffees and finger-chips.

'Yes Anuranjini', said Devashish, adjusting his specks, 'Now, you can say all that you ever wanted to tell me.'

'Shiven', began Anuranjini, 'Sorry, Devashish; I just want to know why did you simply leave me and disappear out of my life just the way you had entered? Had I done that big a crime in marrying Rishabh? Tell me. What was my fault?'

'Anuranjini', said Devashish, gazing intently, 'When I left Sangamner and came to Vadodara, after my twelfth boards, I hardly knew anyone here. My parents had ensured me I would make some good friends and that everything will be fine. You came into my life and I finally found solace in you. Do you remember how I used to talk a lot on about Sangamner and my friends there?'

Anuranjini nodded.

'I had a patient ear in you', continued Devashish, 'I have hell of a temper and you are the only person who could soothe me and control me. You were the only person who understood me and knew me so well. You and I shared a common interest and that was Physics. Then, you went to Bengal and came back appearing like some fairy. I knew Rishabh very well and I am sure you too knew. But he said a word that no young guy generally says—"marriage"; a line that sweeps any girl off her feet. I very well remember those three days trying to explain it out to you. When I saw whatever I said made no difference; I quit. I had warned you in the beginning, remember? After I gave you the gifts, the next thing I did was run away from you and your memories. I took admission for Masters in Physics at Dehradun and it was an integrated course. From Dehradun I ran all the way to Frankfurt. I changed my number and exited totally out of your life—out of the life of the only best friend I ever had. I knew you too wanted to do Masters in Physics but after the marriage to

Rishabh I knew you would do something else that would be convenient from the marriage point of view. I have been running away all these years from you Anuranjini but I couldn't run away from myself; that person in me who is still a best friend. When I came over here in Vadodara, I felt strange; as if I had never studied here at all and never stepped in here. I just had three years of my life here and after three years I have been suffering from deep anguish Anuranjini—an unspeakable pain of which I didn't ever tell anyone; a pain with which I have been fighting and running away from all these years.'

Anuranjini's eyes widened and she asked, 'Why was that such a personal loss to you Devashish? We could have remained the same way after marriage too.'

'That is what you think even now and that is what you thought then', said Devashish smiling scornfully, 'You never saw it, did you? Were you expecting something extraordinary out of me— coming on my knees? Anuranjini, I had thought that I would never tell you but now the reason no longer exists. So I am free to tell you everything.'

Anuranjini waited with bated breath.

'I was in love with you', said Devashish, 'I loved you so much that I was afraid of losing you. That is why I never told you what was going on in my mind. I would have never told you, mark my words; never in all of my life.'

Anuranjini's eyes suddenly filled with tears and they splashed down her face. Devashish's heart twisted to see her; *maybe I still love her.*

'Devashish', said Anuranjini, stemming her flow, 'Why didn't you tell me before? You are telling me when it is late for a lifetime already. Why?'

Now it was Devashish's turn to feel a bit surprised.

'I thought' said Anuranjini, 'That you never felt anything for me. I too loved you then. But then I thought that you really weren't interested in me. When Rishabh showed interest I could not help myself but get drawn by him and I felt I had fallen in love with him. You are right—I was young and reckless and maybe marriage is something no guy ever commits to in such a young age. That probably swept me off my feet more so. If not you, I now feel I should have taken the initiative.'

Devashish gaped at her open-mouthed. Anuranjini's tears came forward with double speed and she wept silently, gasping in between. Devashish wanted to comfort her, say something so that she would stop crying. He could never bear her tears.

'I am happy at least I could tell you all that was going on in my heart and mind', said Devashish.

'So am I.'

After a long minute's pause,

'Anuranjini', he said sadly, 'It is just too late. I am engaging to another girl this Friday. We were the best of friends and that is what it is meant to be. I don't think we were ever destined to carry on as each other's better halves.'

Anuranjini asked, 'Who is she?'

'Meera', replied Devashish, 'My parents' friend's daughter. She is studying Mass Communication. Tell me, why are you so badly affected by this news? You married to Rishabh, the most sought after guy of our own times.'

'That is the only thing the world knows', smiled Anuranjini sadly, 'Including you. I got divorced to Rishabh just yesterday. It is over with him too. He coaxed me to do MBA and that is what I did. After my placement in Ahmadabad, we got married. Initially, it was all fun and nice but after some time; he could not see anything good in me. He criticized me for everything that I did. I tried making adjustments and improvements but it only grew worse. A year back or more, he finally said what was on his mind. He demanded a divorce and ever since I have lost my sleep and diet. The old Rishabh took form and fell in love with another girl, Madhvi whom he is marrying this Thursday. He also tainted my character saying that I was having an affair with you. Others don't even know that for the sake of this marriage you and I had broken our friendship six years back. He had also come to the office canteen and created scene and that is how my office mates came to know about our divorce. He ruined my life completely leaving me with nothing. How much I had wished then that I too had done something in Physics. That would have at least given me a satisfaction that I had not entirely acted on his instructions. Gosh! I loved and still do love Physics.'

Devashish's mouth was partially open. It now explained everything; her tired and bedraggled look and her tears. Devashish wished he could do something. He knew that he couldn't. The helplessness choked him. He didn't like it when all his ways got closed and he was rendered without choice.

'Devashish', she said after a long breather, 'I don't know if I have a right or not. But I wish to meet you and Meera on Thursday before your engagement on Friday. I just want to give you both your wedding presents. Just like you had fulfilled your duty; now it is my turn. Please do allow me. I also want to meet that lucky girl Meera who is marrying my best friend.'

These words of Anuranjini shook Devashish's entire spine. He could see the helplessness on Anuranjini's face and felt very bad.

He paused for a moment and then said, 'Yes Anuranjini. We will meet in front of the University gate overlooking the Sayajigunj Road—our usual, daily entry and exit. I hope you remember. That is the place where it all started Anuranjini when you had grabbed me from going off to the lecture and had screamed at me for being over-smart.'

Anuranjini nodded smiling suddenly. Devashish and Anuranjini sat there a long time talking about other random topics.

Both felt the same thing; *some things never change. If we could not marry each other at least we can remain buddies.*

✷✷✷✷✷✷✷✷✷✷✷✷✷✷✷✷✷✷✷✷✷✷✷✷

#30

On Thursday morning, Anuranjini went to a gift shop to buy gifts for two people—Devashish and Meera. Though she didn't know Meera, she knew a small token on behalf of Devashish's friend would be okay. She seemed too busy and Supriya too noticed that though Anuranjini was tired, she was actually humming a tune as she gift wrapped the presents. She opened her cupboard to take tape and found something that interested her. She took that too.

Anuranjini had to meet Devashish and Meera at around 6.00 PM in front of the MSU gate. She dressed up very consciously and made sure she looked okay and not a bedraggled, tired person.

The party plot Rishabh had booked was resplendent with color and decorations of his choice and he was just too much in the air due to happiness. Madhvi was looking very pretty too and he could barely take his eyes off her. He was quite sure this time he had made no mistake in choosing Madhvi and that he wanted to go on for his entire life with her.

Just this one best decision of my life; thought Rishabh smiling.

Anuranjini drove her vehicle to the decided destination. Since she didn't want to cross in the peak crowd hours at 6.00 pm in the evening, she decided to park her vehicle at the parking lot of the complex opposite to the University on the other side of the road.

When she parked her vehicle and turned, she saw Devashish and a young woman. She seemed very pretty from this distance itself. *Oh God!* Sighed Anuranjini; *She looks beautiful and amazing. Meera is very good. May she and Devashish have a nice life ahead!*

Rishabh's party folks had all arrived and there was merry making. Chosen and selected members of his office and close friends of school and college had arrived. There also was a lawyer friend of his who had come to officially conduct the proceedings. It was not a grand celebration; just a quiet and peaceful yet an energetic and enthusiastic party.

The crowd on this particular road seemed to swell with each passing minute. With great difficulty Anuranjini balancing her three gifts crossed the road in front of her and reached the road divider. She paused for a minute. Devashish hinted out if he should cross and come but Anuranjini shook her head no. She knew if she didn't muster up, she would stand there the whole evening. That is the specialty of Sayajigunj—the peak hours seemed to be generating traffic on its own.

What happened next all came to Devashish's vision in a kind of blur and slow motion. Anuranjini leapt onto the road making sure it was empty or at least that is what she thought she saw but out of the blue, a white company bus with blue-purple stripes came. One minute she was standing there on the road; the other minute she was hurled meters into the air. There was a look of pure terror as the gifts flew out of her hand and she landed with a bone crunching thud on the road. As soon as the bus touched her skin a voice shrieked 'Shiven!' and a parallel 'Andy!' rent the air.

Anuranjini landed on the road and was lying in a pool of her own blood; withering and shivering as her bones were shattered by the effect of the bus running over.

Rishabh and Madhvi came forward towards the small risen platform so that they could all start with the official proceedings for the party. The green grass was a bit wet and it seemed to tingle Madhvi's toes as she walked towards the papers; arm in arm with Rishabh. The signing of papers was important as it was the reason for hoisting this get together at all.

Devashish came running forward along with Meera. The traffic had temporarily frozen on the road. There was a huge block and people gathered around.

'Andy', he said patting her lightly on her cheek, 'Andy stay awake. Andy, look at me. Andy, I am Shiven. Open your eyes.'

Hazily, she opened her eyes and tried to bring both of them into focus. One of the onlookers rushed forward with some water which Devashish tipped into her mouth lightly as she gulped it with difficulty. Her head was in his lap and all three were in her blood-pool.

Rishabh signed the papers that were lying on the table in front of his lawyer friend. Everyone clapped. Then he handed the pen over to Madhvi who was smiling ear to ear. She pushed her hair back as she bent to sign the papers. Her smile couldn't be stopped at all.

'Promise me', she said gasping for breath, 'Promise me you will take all of my presents. You have to; especially the one in red.'

Who the heck cares for the presents— Anuranjini was on a thin thread oscillating between life and death! How could she in this moment mention the gifts!

She turned to Meera and said, 'You are a very good girl. Please take care of Shiven. May God bless you both and you have a nice life ahead.'

Meera's eyes were flooding with tears.

'No Andy', said Devashish, tears running down his face, 'Please don't say like that. An ambulance is on its way.'

'I have not slept in all these months Shiven', said Anuranjini, her eyes beginning to droop, 'Please take my presents as a token of gratitude that you have forgiven me so that I can sleep eternally in peace Shiven; let me sleep! Will always Love . . .' Possibly Anuranjini could never complete those words as the last gust of wind blew out of her lungs, rendering her body still and lifeless.

'Congratulations', announced the lawyer, 'You both are officially declared as husband and wife! May God bless this beautiful couple!'

Everybody clapped and hooted as the two smiled and waved to the guests in the party. They got down the platform and Meera's parents came forward and hugged their son-in-law and daughter. They were very happy for their daughter.

As the words ended, Anuranjini didn't move a muscle. Devashish's face contorted in horror. Anuranjini had died in his arms. There seemed to be now no solution. There was just one fact Devashish knew; *one of the inseparable duo was no more! Out of the coolest pair of "Andy-Shiven", Andy had waved goodbye.*

My Andy has finally slept God; you took her away so that she could peacefully sleep.

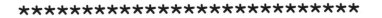

#31

The next day the news papers as well as local news channels carried the news of the incident. There were lots of phone calls and rush going on around.

Vishwas was shocked and shattered when he read the news. When he reached Anuranjini's residence; he could not control his tears at the sight of her condition. Shweta had fully burst into uncontrollable tears.

Nimesh and Vani had lost words and expressions when they had heard the news. When Nimesh went to office, there was a two-minute silence in Anuranjini's memory.

'Friends' addressed the Team Leader at the office, 'Anuranjini was a prized employee and a great human. Unfortunately for us, we lost a gem forever as she left for her heavenly journey. All we can do is pray for her so that wherever she is; she is happy and her soul rests in peace.'

Nimesh was so numb with grief that he had put a one week notice not to attend office.

Parita was not even ready to believe when she got the news. She didn't feel it was real. *How can it be;* she thought; *only few weeks back I had met her.* But the sight of her dead body brought back everything and she was beyond explanation.

Devashish and Meera had postponed their engagement. Devashish was so devastated beyond words that it was more than forty-eight hours since he spoke a single word. He was shell shocked and so much distraught that every single minute he had relived every moment he had spent with Anuranjini—cursing himself for having let go of her. Though Meera didn't know Anuranjini personally, the sight itself was so alarming that she became very quiet and was weeping in one corner of her home and didn't speak to anyone for few days and was constantly by Devashish's side.

Madhvi was shell shocked when she got the news and didn't know how to react. She knew she could not go to Rishabh for solace but she herself had wept uncontrollably. It was as if she had always known Anuranjini and her death came as a shock to her.

Rishabh and his family too weren't feeling any different. Rishabh felt very guilty when he read the news because he internally felt that had it not been for him, Anuranjini would never have reached this condition. He knew he was responsible and yet he didn't have that much courage to go and face her parents. Nevertheless, he went to pay obituary. *It is too late;* he thought; *I promise I will never meddle with anyone's life god. I have done enough damage to one person. Please forgive me Anuranjini; I am truly sorry.*

That one accident seemed to have shocked the entire city of Vadodara and the news constantly was

in the limelight for variety of reasons; sometimes
for the crowd of the university, sometimes for
the traffic hazardous roads, sometimes for a new
parallel diversion for heavy vehicles so that they
didn't hinder the internal roads. It was a talk on
everyone's lips for more than a month at the end
of which it turned into a topic of mere discussion.
Just as life moved on, the incident was going to be
part of the soil and remain there but very soon was
going to be forgotten but fresh in the hearts and
minds of people related to it.

God, called out Devashish, *please take care of
my best friend—she is with you.*

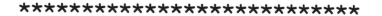

Epilogue

Frankfurt, Germany; Nineteen years later.

'Mommy', called out a young girl of about fourteen, 'Daddy, please come here fast.'

Devashish Shastri and Meera Shastri went running at the call of their daughter's voice.

'Yes Andy', said Devashish, 'What is it?'

'I got an old photo of yours', said the young girl named Andy holding up a frame, 'But mommy is not with you.'

'Anusuya', said Mrs. Meera Shastri sternly, 'I have told you not to mess around with things.'

'Sorry mommy', said Anusuya, 'But I accidentally bumped into it. Whose photo is it anyway?'

'It is daddy's and his best friend's', said Devashish Shastri smiling, 'Do you like it?'

'The auntie is very cute', said Anusuya smiling, 'Can I meet her?'

Meera and Devashish paused to stare at her. Then Devashish smiling at his daughter said,

'I am afraid you cannot meet her. She stays very far away.'

Anusuya looked disappointed.

'Well', said Devashish, 'Do you want an ice cream with a tour of the mall? How about a little shopping?'

Anusuya brightened up and keeping the photo frame haphazardly went to change for the outing. Devashish took the photo frame and stared at the picture in it. It was his and Anuranjini's after they had won the last quiz competition.

Now I will never give you. Keep on begging.

Promise me you will take all of my presents. You have to; especially the one in red.

When he had opened up the red parcel, he had found the photo duly framed and there had not been a single scratch on it even after falling from such a height. It had been properly wrapped in bubble-wrap.

Anuranjini; said Devashish sighing deeply; *you are always with me. I hope you are sleeping peacefully.*